The Island Stood Still

Praise for Michele M. Green

and **THE ISLAND STOOD STILL**

"Thoroughly enjoyed *The Island Stood Still* as Molly Hanson, armed with her Wonder Woman bracelets and a tall glass of wine in hand, brings the nefarious to justice."   *–Bradley and Lana Birge*

"Kookie Molly Hanson is at it again as solving another mystery in her island community. *The Island Stood Still* is truly a fun read. The plot and characters are well-developed and the story is playfully written. This novel easily held my attention. What a great escape. I highly recommend it."   *–Sara Domerchie*

"A delightful entertaining read filled with colorful characters and intriguing local lore. Michele Green's descriptions made me wish I could visit and explore."   *–Deborah G. Baltimore, MD*

"Michele Green is brilliant at crafting a mystery. Fast-paced and wickedly funny. Irresistible! If you like Lisa Scottoline, you will love the Molly Hanson series."   *–Heidi Thompson*

"*The Island Stood Still* was a book I could not put down. Looking forward to the next in the series."   *–Martha Mister*

"Who wouldn't love Molly Hanson as a best friend? She solves mysteries, defies authority and drinks wine well before 5pm! A true trifecta!"   *–Dianne Smith*

The Island Stood Still

Michele M. Green

NEW YORK

BLUEBERRY
LANE BOOKS

Michelegreen.net

Blueberrylanebooks.com

Cover photo by Michele M. Green

Photograph of author with her dog Sara Jane by Jay Fleming Photography.

Cover design by Kevin Michaels

ISBN: 978-1-942183-20-4

I have dedicated The Island Stood Still to those of you

who believed in me.

And to those of you who didn't, you were wrong.

-prologue-

Roaring along three short blocks, the diesel engine choked and rattled to a rocking halt, spoiling the dreamy repose of the tree-lined suburban neighborhood. The cab's rusty metal door moaned as it swung open and the driver slid from the vehicle with shoulders braced against the brisk air. He stood bathed in spears of sunlight falling through dormant tree branches, scraping his leather boot along the pavement, brushing a trail of crumbling cement crumbs aside. He didn't mind waiting. He was a patient man.

Consumed in their idle banter, two high school girls floated down the sidewalk on autopilot drawing nearer to the man.

Too easy, he thought, stepping into view. The girls hesitated. Their airy conversation ceased. The man extended his palm, revealing a small item, something he knew they wanted. He nodded towards the lumbering vehicle and the girls climbed inside. And then, the man drove them away.

one

"Oh no, not again," I groaned, rolling over in the bed, trying to ignore the vibrating cell phone shimmying across the nightstand. I recognized the annoying pings as another Amber Alert notice, the second one this week. The thought created a strange prickling along the surface of my arms. Even though I wasn't officially in law enforcement, my curiosity and skewed sense of judgement have led me into precarious situations that luckily end well.

Struggling with the oversized T-shirt twisted around my waist, I hoisted my half-asleep body on elbows and tapped the phone, squinting the tiny text lettering into focus.

I can't function properly at this unfortunate hour. It's not that I mind starting the day early, as long as I don't have to do anything useful like read a public announcement written in a font set for a field mouse.

Fifteen-year-old female reported missing. Last seen in the vicinity of Oakwood approximately six-forty-five this morning.

I knew the statistics. The first seventy-two hours are the most critical. It's an insanely small window that authorities have to locate missing persons alive. It's understood that persons in this particular age bracket generally disappear of their own volition, often returning within a day. This girl fits the bill, a young hormonal teenager who most likely left home after an argument with her parents. I tell myself there's no need to emotionally involve myself any further. This has absolutely nothing to do with me. The responsibility of finding that girl belongs to the authorities alone. I refuse to allow these texts to inhabit any more precious real-estate in my mind.

The morning light beamed through the window sheers with such a harsh intensity it formed a dull headache behind my eyes. Knowing I needed a caffeine fix before it turned into a full-blown migraine, I ventured downstairs to the kitchen where the dogs waited patiently by the back door. I let them outside for a pee in the cold salt-thickened air. Humidity on the island is constant, more so in winter.

Taking my Wonder Woman mug from the cabinet, I filled it with leftover coffee still hot from the pot and lifted the dark brew to my lips, tasting the stale bitterness. Hank never remembers to turn off the pot, no matter how often I tell my husband that the house is going to burn to the ground, and the insurance company will refuse compensation because the house fire was all his fault.

My headache pounded harder, increasing in rhythm as if trying to escape my skull using a jackhammer. Fishing through the cabinet for some sort of pain reliever, I swallowed four aspirins that were sure to burn a hole through my stomach within the hour.

This routine has become a fairly familiar one I hate to admit aloud. I'd rather blame the headache on anything feasible other than wine. On more than one occasion, Hank had thought it necessary to express his opinion on the volumes of wine I consume by saying, *Molly Hanson, one of these days you're going to drown yourself,* which is an exaggeration of course. I'd never waste wine if I poured it into my lungs.

Sometimes, after my second or third glass of wine, I say it's my last. But come morning, I usually forget all about any such pledge. I sincerely doubt I possess the willpower necessary to abstain from alcohol, but with the aid of the current headache, I made a mental sticky note to cut back on consumption.

Hank came in through the back door bringing a blast of cold with him, and the dogs tagging along, vying for his attention. He tossed them a dog treat, then kissed the top of my head as if I were a child. He smelled of saltwater and marsh mud.

"Hey Molly, didn't expect you to be up and about."

"How did you do this morning?" I answered in a yawn because it was incredibly laborious to appear engaged this early.

"Six bushels of oysters. Not bad for a couple of hours. Would have liked to have stayed out longer, but I got a full day ahead of me."

Hank works for the Maryland Department of Natural Resources in Wildlife Management by winter's day, and as a seasonal waterman on summer mornings. He's up working the water for his bushel limit of crabs before the birds even think about singing. His winter months are spent banding Canadian geese, managing invasive plant species, or creating animal food plots, and he can make a mean breakfast for the boys at work. He's constantly on the move, so much so that I believe he might instantaneously implode if he stayed still for too long.

"What's on your agenda today?" Hank asked in his perpetual upbeat lilt that would get on my nerves if he wasn't so handsome.

"Setting the world on fire," I replied, clearing the morning from my throat.

"Try and stay out of trouble while you're at it."

"What's the fun in that?" But in reality, what trouble could I get into living on an island that had a total population of nine residents of mostly watermen, and two dogs? In Smithtown, our house is located beyond the vanishing point at the far end of the marsh where surprisingly, passports are not required to enter. The town is immune to outside world influences such as Netflix, which makes one's existence about as exciting as watching the grass grow. On the island, life is slowed, electricity is intermittent at best, and the internet is something dreams are made of. Long ago forgotten by the outside world, Smithtown remains untouched by time, sometimes I believe on purpose. How anyone was able to find this tiny blot on the map without the aid of a search party is purely a miracle.

"See you tonight, hon." Hank grabbed his wad of office keys from the wall hook, then kissed my head again. I'd hate to think the pizazz had fizzled already from our marriage. Maybe if I start brushing my teeth first thing, I'd get a kiss on the lips.

Hearing the front door slam closed, I rested my head in my hands listening to Hank's truck rumble over the three bridges leading to the mainland until it faded into the distance. It's another day with nothing to do and all day to do it. Wait a minute. Did that text say the girl was missing from Oakwood? It's considered to be a fairly safe neighborhood, mostly new builds with manicured lawns and playgrounds. How could this happen in a reputable place like that? Her parents must be devastated, especially with the Christmas holiday right around the corner.

Once more I opened the text app on my phone and scrolled through the messages revisiting an Amber Alert sent two days ago. I noticed they were alarmingly similar, both female, around the same age, and reported missing within close proximity. Perhaps the girls decided to play hooky and were having the time of their lives in Ocean City. I can remember back in my day when I did my fair share of skipping classes. Eventually, the school decided to award me with a diploma in hopes it would keep me from ever returning. Unfortunately, life is so much scarier now and the predators are more prevalent, even in the nicer neighborhoods.

I picked up the grimy remote belonging to the television Hank insists on having in the kitchen, and pressed the red button. The news reporter's salon tanned face materialized across much of the screen and caused me to lean back in the chair.

A third Somerset County juvenile is reported missing and was last seen this morning on her way to Somerset High School. Authorities are asking for any information leading to her whereabouts. Up next, your local weather report after a word from our sponsor.

In less time than it takes for the human heart to beat, the reporter had transformed his persona from empathetic despair to an optimistic buoyancy, which made me wonder if he secretly practiced facial expressions in the bathroom mirror. Though I quickly shut the television off, it did little to eliminate the disturbing news niggling around my edges, eating its way to the forefront of my attention.

The reporter mentioned three young women missing. It could be just random events without any connection between them. But there's something about the situation that feels off, I thought, and my intuition is never wrong. I just need to remind myself this is none of my concern and maintain a stronghold on my obsessive tendencies before I'm pulled down another bottomless rabbit hole.

Who am I kidding? I knew those Amber Alerts were not a random coincidence, and that there was way more to this story than what the media was telling. I also knew there was little chance I would let it go.

- *two* -

Two cups of old coffee later, my hands trembled more than a California earthquake, and the aspirin burning my stomach lining into a new queasy shape made me feel like crap. Foraging about the kitchen, I found a box of saltines on the high shelf in the pantry, perfect to soak up the acids. Our kitchen is old like the rest of the house that leaks cold air through its shrunken seams. The cabinets were built onsite around the mid-fifties, while the linoleum flooring, though yellowed over the years, is completely intact, and the ceiling fan operates with one good smack. The gas stove is probably carbon dated to the stone age, and lighting the thing is the most terrifying death-defying feat I have ever done.

The view beyond the back window to the marsh creek is unaltered, as is the front. The stunning experience of the sunrise renders my endurance of the vintage room worthwhile. The island is constantly evolving. There is a drastic shift in the landscape occurring at an invisible line where salt intolerant animals turn back from the rich green earth of the mainland for the freshwater and tall grassy fields.

With a fistful of saltines in hand, I left the kitchen and headed for the front room with the dogs faithfully tagging behind, scarfing up a trail of cracker crumbs. Passing by the hall mirror, I caught a glimpse of my sun spackled hair, a wreck as usual. I am taller than most women, with no fashion sense what-so-ever, and will forever have dirt permanently infused beneath my fingernails. Except for the hair, my likeness is patterned after my father, thin build with an angular face. The only difference being his hair was dark and held neatly in place by a black plastic comb he kept secured in his pocket. I miss my parents and wish more than anything they were still alive. I wish I could be more like them, generous, kind, and selfless in nature. But if wishes were horses, I would ride to the end of the universe only to end up on Smithtown Island again. Okay, maybe Smithtown isn't exactly the end of the world, but if you keep walking past the road's end and continue over the marsh and beyond the Tangier Sound, you just might fall into oblivion.

The front part of our antiquated shore house faces the Sound where I can easily lose myself staring out one of the four large windows, each with an equally breath-taking view of life on the water in the sharp concentrated hues of winter light. The air, thin and crisp, brings watermen dredging for oysters deceivingly close.

For most of December, the island temperatures had remained in an abnormally balmy state. Bits of bright green sprouted with hope between the brown blades of lawn grass. Miraculously, Smithtown seems to have escaped the vicious marrow-biting winds that tear across the landscape reforming the contours. It would be fine by me if winter passed without notice. I prefer the summer flip-flop season. Or not wearing shoes of any kind. I've been like that since I was small, and I can remember countless conference calls home about my bare feet in the classroom. My mother never reprimanded my shoeless behavior, or chided me when my father drove his Dodge Dart over the

Barbie I carelessly left in the driveway. The doll's deformity made no difference to me. I continued hurling her through the air so she could fly like Wonder Woman.

If only I could wave a magic wand and return to my childhood where everything was pure and simple and right as rain. But that was once upon a time in a faraway land where I ran wild in the suburbs of Trenton, New Jersey, a place where pork roll meats were king in the smog filled air, peopled with the most durable creatures on the planet. That kind of childhood is what made me who I am today. Molly Hanson, New Jersey bad-ass.

My cell buzzed, abruptly dislodging the walk down memory lane, something I found myself doing often lately. I read the number displayed across the screen and let it go to voicemail. It takes a certain amount of perseverance in dealing with my sister. It's been more than a year since our mother passed, and yet Megan insists on inserting her death into nearly every conversation. I miss my mother the same as Megan does. But memories of her, even the sweetest, generates a suffocating pain radiating from the center of my chest. I find it's easier to block all remembrances like they never existed. Despite the effort, recall loiters at the sidelines of my mind, surfacing without warning. Life continues to roll on, no matter what's hurled in your path. I had moved on for my own preservation. Hank had the right idea when he polished off the bereavement cake hidden in the freezer behind the frozen vegetables. His sweet tooth has a mind of its own regardless of how pitiful the occasion.

There's a six-year age difference between me and my sister, which seemed like light years at first. Megan was the source of perfection in my parent's eyes. She reveled in her only child status until I was born. We shared a bedroom on the second floor where Megan pressed her pillow tightly over my face every night. Though Megan's nightmarish reign of terror is behind me now, it's still difficult to muster even the smallest ounce of empathy towards her. When Sunday morning comes, I pray for my sister. As far as the rest of the week goes, she's on her own.

Bound by blood, I feel plagued by a sense of family duty. We are unified in sorrow, scaling rough terrain over the majestic grief mountains of New Jersey. I know at some point I'll have to forgive my sister, forgiveness accomplished from afar. Very far.

My stomach gurgled in pangs of hunger for something more than a few crackers. Returning to the kitchen to rifle the vintage cabinets for nourishment that didn't require any real effort to prepare, I chose the box of corn flakes reinforced with ingredients I had little desire in learning how to pronounce, then dumped the sugary contents into a bowl. Fetching the milk from the refrigerator, I spied the half bottle of Chardonnay and debated pouring the remainder over the cereal. Daytime drinking sure would make it easier when dealing with my sister. I supposed I could be a better person and return Megan's call. Scrolling through the contacts, my finger hovered over her phone number.

"Forget this. I've got better things worry about," I said and glanced around at the state of chaos. Laundry piled up in the utility room, dishes stacked high in the sink, and dog-hair tumbleweeds floated freely across the floor. Procrastination is one of my formidable skills.

I grabbed the broom leaning in the corner and began wrangling the dirt in a pile when my phone rang again. Overcome by guilt, I answered on the fourth ring.

"Molly, it's me again," Megan said, her voice barely audible over yappy dogs wailing in the background. I always thought her horizontally challenged Chihuahuas looked like bloated ticks on a dog's backside.

"Can you hear me?" I hollered out, regretting answering. Between Megan and those pesky Amber Alerts, I should just pitch the damn cell phone in the marsh.

"Are you there?" Megan's voice wavered.

"Yeah, I'm still here." I couldn't take much more of her crying jags. Losing a parent is a life altering event and it's left me rusted in place like a bike left out in the rain. My cognitive skills congealed into a wad of scrambled eggs and I swallowed the dog's medication by mistake. On the upside, I wouldn't have to worry about a flea infestation breakout.

"Are you busy?" she asked.

I should have said yes and disconnected the call, but it was too late and impossible to avoid her now. "No, it's alright. Good to hear from you," I lied.

"I miss her," she sniveled.

"Me too," I agreed, painfully aware of the pregnant pause holding the line hostage.

"This will be my first Christmas without her. I don't know how I will survive."

"I'm trying to figure that out as well." Strange how I suddenly felt the most unexpectant urge to hug my sister. Any

11

thought of celebrating the holiday had fallen to the bottom of my agenda now that both my parents were out of the picture.

"It's just so hard." Megan said, her voice on the verge of another breakdown.

"Do you think she's still ringing?" I knew the question would cheer her up.

"Probably," Megan's tone perked a notch.

Soon after our mother became ill, she was diagnosed with a horrific and very rare degenerative arthritis disease that eventually bound her to a wheelchair in agony. I couldn't comprehend a reason that would justify her perpetual torment, and that had caused me to question my faith more than once. As the disease progressed, the surgeon inserted a mind-numbing pain medication administering pump in my mother's cavity, filled with everything in the pharmaceutical market strong enough to kill a team of Clydesdale horses. When the device became ineffective in alleviating her excruciating misery, liquid morphine treatments were administered as a palliative care method. Hospice was called in, and the pain pump was turned off. However, the pump ran on a ten-year lithium battery and had an alarm that rang when the pump ran low on pain medication, every hour on the hour. The alarm could only be heard in somber atmospheres like that of a funeral pallor. As bizarre as it seemed, the alarm buzzing during the service launched us both into a full-frontal belly laughing assault. Making fun of grim situations with snarky humor had always been our family coping mechanism, and how I mastered emotional deflection.

"I bet the alarm frightens the graveyard maintenance man."

"You'll rot in hell for mocking our mother," Megan laughed.

"Well, at least I'll be in good company with you seated there next to me."

Megan laughed, gasping for air, "I have to hang up now, my sides are splitting apart. I love you."

"Yep," I answered. Returning the sentiment at this point would give me the willies. We disconnected the call with Megan's spirit slightly mended and mine, slightly heavier as a scene forming in my mind rewound to my mother's casket lowering beneath the ground. My throat tightened into a choking knot. I collapsed to the floor hugging my knees as the dogs licked at my face. Canines seem to have an innate knowledge of knowing the right thing to do.

"I'll be alright," I said, rubbing their heads. Bam's ears twitched towards a sound tenderly rising to a crescendo throughout the house.

"They're here," I shouted, stumbling to my feet and out the back door to see hundreds of long white necks soaring across the wintry sky. Tundra swans migrate from the arctic by the thousands for a short interval on Maryland's eastern shore, taking temporary residency on Piney Island. Their distinct song is part of the music that rises from the marshes, and one of the few things that makes living on the island bearable for me.

The parade of elegant white birds landed on the water undeterred by threatening weather conditions looming overhead. Moving fast, the storm stirred white caps thrashing at the shoreline. I scurried inside when a powerful gust of wind brought a snowsquall, washing the ground in a flurry of white flakes. The first sign of icy conditions to come over the island for months.

The sudden storm forced bitter air to penetrate the window joints and my clothing. I shivered at the chill sliding up my spine. The swing in the weather roused a mournful sentiment drifting towards the murkier spaces in my mind, and turning my mood critical. I checked the time. I had managed to waste the better part of the morning without notice. Needing a change of scenery, I snatched a jacket and the minivan keys from the wall hook, and the tinkling sound sent the dogs bounding for the front door.

Outside, I loaded them into the van and turned the engine on, checking for nonexistent traffic, then backed the vehicle over the driveway listening to the oyster shells pop and splinter under the weight of tires.

I had no idea where I was going, but by the time I passed over the three bridges, I felt my darkened temperament lessen with each mile driven by the swatches of marsh plants undulating into one intricate span of color. I didn't care where I ended up as long as it was completely void of Amber Alerts and thoughts of death lingering overhead. Unfortunately, I knew I had a better chance of shooting a butterfly in a gale wind with a rubber-band slingshot than I did of finding a smidgen of peace.

- *three* -

"Quit it, Bam," I snapped, maneuvering the van into the Gas & Go Mart alongside gas pump number four. The dog had frayed my last nerve bellowing his banshee shrieks and smearing his snotty nose across the windshield the entire ride.

"Why can't you behave like Sara Jane?" I ran my fingers through my black-lab's fur, her body stretched out on the floor of the van. Everyone in Smithtown loves Sara, who stops by the neighbor's whenever she feels a hankering for a visit. Bam, a cattle dog prone to fitful outbursts, with a preference for drinking toilet water and rolling in rancid carcasses, is not as welcomed in neighboring homes.

"That's enough now. Be quiet," I begged, but the howling continued in ear bleeding volume, causing yet another public display. I prepared myself in my usual litany of excuses to those gawking at us.

He's a rescue with separation anxiety issues, returned to the pound three times, and yes, the veterinarian prescribed sedatives that have little effect on the situation unless I swallow them.

I slipped out of the van and closed the door, leaving the shrieking mess of fur behind me, and went inside the store. The Gas & Go Mart was located caddy-corner to the Sheriff's Department that sat next to the Somerset County ball field. The store was a treasure trove of greasy fast-food finds, and also the popular hang-out place for the locally disgruntled unemployed chin-waggers who spend their time discussing the current state of affairs. The Gas & Go Mart kept me supplied in petrol, cheapo-box wine, and occasionally, a three-dollar winning scratch off lottery ticket.

The store was overseen by a Pakistani man named Yusuf, the proprietor of a small chain of Gas & Go Marts that materialized overnight across Maryland. I understand very little about the man, or his culture, and don't wish to learn more. Living in a fishing village on an island with a population grand total of nine people, I get more than enough culture to last me a lifetime. My only knowledge about Yusuf was that he's a pleasant man who takes great effort in remembering his customer's names, even mine. In Somerset County, life was small-town, and maintaining anonymity was downright impossible.

"What's shakin', Yusuf?" I asked, flinging the double glass doors open.

"Same crap, different day, how about you Molly?" He flashed his usual smile of incredibly white teeth. Even though Yusuf spoke with a European accent, he seemed to have the Americana lingo phrasing down with no problem.

"How much gas do you want today?"

"Ten bucks, please." Although I had a twenty-dollar-bill in my pocket, I needed the change for junk food.

Strolling down the snack aisle, my eyes glazed over at the rows of shiny aluminum bags lining shelves filled with heart clogging goodies. I crammed as many as I could in my arms, then headed for the register, plopped my loot on the counter, and grabbed two hotdogs from the rotisserie warmer.

"I see you're on that health kick diet again," Yusuf noted amusedly, while stuffing my loot into plastic Gas & Go Mart monogrammed bags. "You Americans all the same."

I was about to defend my dietary bootie when the store's door opened and in strolled a glassy eyed man with a big goober grin plastered across his face. Obviously, he was stoned. He gave us both a nod, floated down the snack aisle and snatched a large bag of BBQ Kettle Chips.

I noticed Yusuf's altered demeanor, his attention on the stoner guy's car tags. He dug out a pen and got busy writing down the number of the Delaware license plate.

"What's going on?" I asked, but he chose not to answer. I followed Yusuf's line of sight fixed on the stoner guy as he walked right on by us, gave us another nod and left the store with the giant bag of chips as if they were his for the taking.

"Aw you know not. That guy just stole those chips. Are you going to stop him or what?"

"No, I don't chase them for chips anymore, too dangerous."

"But he's stealing your stuff. Isn't that against the law?"

"The loss is absorbed into store pricing," noted Yusef, like it was a normal everyday occurrence.

"I still say it's wrong to take what isn't yours, not to mention it's not fair that I ultimately end up paying for his chips."

"Welcome to America," he offered as an answer for all world problems.

"Maybe you should think about an alarm system. A little artillery behind the counter wouldn't hurt."

"Nothing to get upset about Molly, it's just a bag of chips. I don't shoot no one for chips. Not worth the price of the bullet."

Yusuf probed his hand under the counter and spoke in softened decibels. "Now mess with my money and you got some big surprise coming."

I saw no need in knowing what he had stored under that counter. Whatever it was, most likely it wasn't legal. The less I knew the better. I thought this the best moment to vacate the premises, paid my bill, and gathered up my bags.

"Thanks, Yusuf, see you later," I said, and left the store.

"Say hello to your kind husband for me. You lucky woman, you picked your husband. In my country that never happens. Sometimes the husband is as ugly as a goat." Yusuf continued talking as I crossed the lot. He may be successful at business, but I think the man was a little off and could be missing the cuckoo from his clock.

I finished pumping petrol into the tank and then dispersed snacks of cheesy poofs and hotdogs for my canine passengers, keeping the waffle chips for myself. With a full mouth, I scanned the area for anything interesting to watch. Just the usual unemployed sentinels on guard, not an uncommon sight. Being parked at the pump turned out to be the ideal vantage point for viewing all ports, including an old rusty tan station-wagon rolling out from the driveway of the creepy house across the street from the Sheriff's office.

The wagon's engine revved at a fast clip, sending puffs of smoke floating sideways via vintage eight-cylinders that must cost a small fortune to run. The car flew into the lot on two wheels, almost slamming into the glass storefront before stopping. I heard shouts erupt inside the wagon, then a young woman jumped out from the car with a man hurrying after her. He grabbed at her arm, catching her above the elbow. The woman shook loose and then shoved him away.

Livid, he screamed at his fleeing passenger, "Go on then you whore, good riddance." The man was dressed in an oversized camouflage hoodie, and appeared too inappropriately old to be her significant other. He climbed inside the wagon, then screeched tires through the lot, exiting onto the highway. My days are usually conducted without any sense of direction at all, but this day was picking up momentum. Pairing entertainment with a junk food binge couldn't be any better than this, unless the show included wine.

Clearly agitated, the girl stamped her feet, weaving among the multitude of parked cars. She seemed anxious, or possibly it was desperation I saw in her search. The girl spotted my figure in the van, came nearer and then banged on the side window. She flew back a few paces when Bam's head popped up.

"What the hell was that you got in there, a rabid raccoon?" she questioned, alarmed at the sight of him.

The girl was thin as a rail, with medium length dirty-blonde hair, and much younger than what I originally surmised. She might have been fifteen, or even as old as nineteen, I couldn't tell for sure. She wore a pair of jeans and a long sleeve navy-blue shirt sporting a rock band logo across the chest, not enough clothing to stave off the cold.

"Do you have a dollar?"

"Sure, hold on a sec," I answered, digging through the ash tray for coins. "Kinda chilly to be out here without a coat. Where are you heading?" I handed her the money through the window.

"That's none of your business," she answered, filling her pocket with the loose change, then hurried off.

"You're welcome!" I grumbled. The girl, besides being versed in the art of scrounging for money, had given me the impression something wasn't kosher about this pickle. I could only imagine what sort of activity she's involved in with that guy from the creepy house. No good, I was certain of it.

Having my fill of junk food, I tossed the last of the cheesy puffs to the dogs, turned the van's engine over, then pulled out onto old route four-thirteen. As entertaining as the Gas & Go Mart show was, I had to go home. The sky, now a muddy gray, was hastening towards the night. I find driving at night impossible since the salt air etches the plastic headlight covers to a dulled yellow surface which makes navigating route four-thirteen terrifying. Streetlights are nonexistent, and the six-foot deep drainage ditches lining the sides of the curvy road add to the hazardous drive. The road department never bothered installing guardrails along the dicey pavement, and in several places it's quite the heart stopping drop over the side. On the upside, the ditches preserve the Somerset Towing company's gainful employment.

Up in the distance I saw a blur of movement on the left side of the road. Most likely a herd of deer fleeing across the ground. I took precautions, flicking on the high beams for optimal visibility, though I saw no change through the hazy plastic. But by now I could see it was one shape. Cautiously, I approached the object, creeping along until certain the figure was the girl from the Gas & Go Mart trudging ahead.

"Aw you know not!" Walking this road in the daytime was dangerous enough, let alone at night. Easing up on the gas pedal, I pulled over and opened the window "Where are you going? Do you need a lift?"

The girl looked up and down the empty road debating her reply. As the sun set, the temperature was dropping with it. It would be a miserable walk wherever she happened to be heading. The cold air had taken hold, shaping her response.

"Yes, I guess I do." Lacking options, the girl cautiously opened the door and pushed Bam out of the passenger's seat. He planted his tongue in her mouth before moving.

"Get down Bam. Sorry, he likes to do that to people. Where are you heading?" I quizzed her again, but she didn't answer. No, she refused to answer. Suspicion rose in my gut. I looked over the girl before putting the van in gear. Not only was she thin, but her skin seemed paler in color, as if she was malnourished. I decided she was pitiful but harmless. "This is a very dangerous road to walk at night. And you should wear proper protection in this kind of weather."

"I'm fine," the girl grunted as she glared at me.

"I suppose it's not necessary to be reminded of the dangers of hitching rides, especially for young women like yourself. There are way too many wacky doodles in this world if you ask me. People turn up missing every day you know."

"I didn't ask, and by the way, you can't 'turn up' if you're missing," she snarked. Her sardonic, disgusted tone centered her age closer to sixteen or seventeen. The only experience I had with teenage angst had come from my sister. That's what teenagers do, making sure everyone within earshot was miserable before leaving home to forge a life of their own. This girl reminded me of my dealings with Megan, and her state of affairs was undeniably the reason why I stopped the van in the first place.

"Scary bad stuff happens everywhere. In fact, I just heard a news story about an ordinary girl, like you, who had simply vanished from the school's cafeteria. Where's your family located? Is there someone I should call? Shouldn't you be home doing your homework?"

"Ordinary? Did I hear you call me ordinary? Screw you lady! You sound like my mother. I don't need a rash of crap or anything else you're selling! Who do you think you are anyway? Stop this car and let me out!"

"But it's nightfall, and much colder now," I said, slowing the car.

"You're a genuine whack job, you know that? Let me out of this car now."

The van had barely come to a halt when the girl bolted from the door and high-tailed it up the road towards the Gas & Go Mart. I felt an overwhelming desire to protect this girl, but from what, I didn't know. I cried out, "Wait, wait, come back. I can take you where you need to go." With a sense of helplessness, I watched the girl in the rearview mirror ingested by darkness. *No good deed goes unpunished.*

I drove the remnants of the route towards home with a feeling of unease growing inside me, and flashes of the angry girl weighing even heavier on my mind. I'm not quite sure of what happened, except that the exchange was definitely weird. There was something off about the girl, a sense of desperation behind her tough-as-nails act. I thought the odds of those Amber Alerts being somehow connected to this particular girl were higher than outer space. My stomach sickened as a metallic taste began to rise up my throat.

- f our -

Entering the front door to our home, I heard strange, unfamiliar sounds spewing from deep within. Stranger still, were the delicious house-saturating aromas. When I realized it was Hank in the kitchen preparing dinner, a great relief washed over me knowing I wouldn't have to conjure up some sort of food for us. I hate cooking.

"Hi hon," Hank smiled. "Did I tell you Walt will be joining us tonight? We're eating deer steaks, smashed potatoes with gravy, and real fresh green beans, not the mushy canned green beans that leave that weird metal taste in your mouth. He's on his way. Hope that's alright with you?"

"Sure, as long as I don't have to acknowledge Sheriff Jerk-face," I replied, hanging my coat by the door and wrapping my arms around my husband who was like pure oxygen to me. From time to time, most marriages hit a rough patch in the road becoming disjointed for a while, calling upon a great effort to piece it back together. Regardless of how upset or annoyed Hank is with me, I will always run to the safe haven of his arms.

"Nice to see you home from work early," I said. My husband is adored by everyone, including animals, unless he's hunting one for dinner. Hank is one-hundred percent *Manly Man*, who often leaves a ripe pineapple in the fridge just to surprise me.

"What's up? You look a little harried," he asked, his eyes fixed on the state of my hair. I ran my hand over my head smoothing the wayward strands and my fingers became tangled.

"There's nothing about my day worth repeating." That was not my first lie of the day, but totally necessary. Hank works too hard to hear about my daily foolish antics.

The old landline wall-phone rang out, making me thankful for the interruption. We keep the phone active in case of an electrical outage. On the island, electric shortages occur weekly and the inconvenient pattern hadn't changed since they first installed power lines in nineteen-forty-seven. I know Smithtown isn't the end of the world, but it seems as though technology has abandoned this town wrapped in a blanket on a time-warped doorstep.

The second ring sent the phone crashing to the floor. The startling noise set the dogs running to hide in the safety of the bedroom.

"I'll get it," I said, annoyed. "I'm not sure why we have this old thing. It's mostly solicitors that call anyway," I sighed, balancing the jumbled phone mess in my arms. "Hello?"

"Is Denise there?" inquired a male voice from the other end. "I have a very special offer."

"Denise? No, De-nise isn't here, but de-nephew is," I answered, slamming down the receiver.

Hank rolled his eyes, "Maybe we should get rid of that thing."

"You think? These calls get worse by the day. I swear if I get one more irritating call, I'm sticking my head in the oven. Did you ever wonder how many people actually committed suicide as a direct result of robo call harassment. The calls are nothing but sales people trying to sell exotic travel packages, vacation time-shares and Viagra prescriptions, which would be fine if I wanted to take my enhanced penis on a holiday," I paused, taking a deep breath. "Is it wine o'clock yet?"

"Molly, what's wrong? Don't tell me you're thinking about saving the world again?" Hank asked, pouring the remaining chardonnay into a wine glass then handed it to me, which I took to like a baby duck to the water.

"It's Megan. She's having difficulty accepting the fact that our mom is dead. I wish I could help her, but I can't. She doesn't consider how hard it is for me." In two gulps the wine glass was empty. I debated whether I should tell him that it was the Amber Alerts and that girl from Gas & Go Mart that was bothering me. I would wait to mention it over dinner. It might spur Walt into cop mode, making him spill the official inside department scoop.

"First of all, you can't wave a wand and make it all better. And secondly, be patient and give your sister some space. She'll come around." Hank placed his arms around my shoulders, squeezing all my problems away. "You'll see," he said softly.

"If only I could believe that were true."

"Trust me. Everything will be fine." Hank pulled away to look me in the eyes. His face, so beautiful and sincere, I could almost believe it.

There are circumstances that would make any couple question the concept of marriage. My marriage wasn't one of them. Yusuf was right, I am lucky I didn't marry a goat. I made a mental note to appreciate my husband more often from now on.

Michele M. Green

- five -

"I'll get it," I said. The doorbell's musical sequence summoned the dogs' attention, bounding for the front room. I pushed them aside and opened the door for Walter, Hank's best friend and local sheriff, who stood there filling the door frame.

They met each other on the water years ago, during a routine boat inspection when Walter was employed by the natural resource police. They discovered they both had a passion for sport fishing, and much to my dismay have been best friends ever since. Walter joined the sheriff's department six months after his retirement from the NRP, and now serves eviction notices, often transporting the evictees to county shelters during the colder months. My husband acts like Walter's the next best thing since fortified white bread. My first impression, the man appeared all soft and gooey like a big teddy bear, but experience has shown him to be a colossal horse's ass who has a weighted shapelessness about him from a not-so-secret Tasty Cake obsession, and bears a strong resemblance to Mr. Potato Head. For some unknown reason, Hank seems to have held their friendship dear from the very first, and has been cultivating their bro-mance ever since. Even though we can't stand being in the same room, I tolerate Sheriff Fat-man's invasion for my husband's sake alone. Hank does his best to ignore us both.

"Smells fantastic, Hank must be cooking," he grinned, proving my point about his ass-status.

"Come on in, Walt. Hank is in the kitchen. Can I get you a beer?" I asked, feigning my way through the niceties.

Walt flung his hat on the coat rack only to be forgotten as usual on his way out. "Sure, but it's for medicinal purposes, mind you. My feet are bothering me today. Must be the cold."

"Isn't that the same reason you use each time you stuff anything inside your mouth?" I lowered my eyes at Walter's ever widening mid-section.

"I didn't realize I was such a fascinating topic to you. Never mind that. Why don't you be a good girl and fetch me that beer?"

"Bite me." I flipped Walter the bird. "Get it yourself," I said, heading for the kitchen. Walter scrambled past, bumping me against the hallway and burst into the kitchen first. Like I said, the only thing Walter and I share in common is our mutual interest in Hank. Our intense dislike for each other is a bonus.

"Hey Walt, glad you made it. Want a beer?" asked Hank, already reaching in the fridge for a cold one.

"You're a good man." Walter twisted the cap off, then tossed it in the sink. "It sure is frigid out there," he added.

"You got that right. The wind whipping across the water doesn't help much." Scooping up a glass tumbler, Hank dropped in several ice cubes, then poured bourbon on top, crackling the ice. "Molly, do you want me to open another bottle of wine?" he asked.

"My answer would have to be a big hell-yes until the day I die and my dead cold fingers can't hold the wine glass anymore."

"I shouldn't have asked." Hank shook his head, then forged through the drawers for a corkscrew.

"I'll have to start relocating people camped out under the bypass bridge to shelters tomorrow," Walter mentioned, making himself at home by sitting down at the table. "They get crowded fast in the winter months. Half of the homeless end up sleeping on the floor. Our church is conducting a blanket drive if you would like to donate to the cause." He took a large swallow from the cold beer, and then another. "Yeah, day after day, the city of Salisbury is full of wandering souls panhandling food money at stoplights."

"That's a sad situation, especially in this weather," Hank replied, swirling the ice cubes in his glass.

"People fall on hard times land in dire straits. Even sadder are the panhandlers working the crowd to support a drug habit. Nobody chooses to live like that."

I poured myself a glass of wine, then joined Walter at the table and knocked back half the contents. Getting through this dinner wouldn't be easy. The wine never fails to save me. "I saw a man at the Walmart parking lot entrance playing an accordion. I listened for a while until security chased him off the property. He had a sign asking for help to feed his family, I gave him four bucks from my wallet, and the change I scrounged from the carpet." Draining the remainder of wine, I got up and refilled the glass to the brim. "Never saw him again."

"You did right. It's best to limit giving money only to those people carrying signs," Hank joined in.

"Why?" I asked, puzzled by his statement.

"Some of them don't want to be bothered. The sign shows when they're approachable. I keep dollar bills in the glove box for sign-people hustling change at the stop lights." Hank swirled the cubes around in the tumbler, then took a sip.

"Good to know." I said, impressed by my husband's generosity.

"Walt, about this blanket drive of yours, we want to donate, or help anyway we can with the cause. I'll tell the fellows at work. I'm sure they'll want to chip in as well."

It came as no surprise that Hank would be the first to pipe up and say something decent. Mr. Goody Two-Shoes was a man of virtue and sheer perfection in all human ways. It's no wonder everyone loves my husband. I'm not like him at all. Instinct tells me I need to come up with an excuse asap, or I'll be stuck shopping for the blankets at Walmart, and those trips rarely end well. Contrary to what Hank believes, I don't enjoy embarrassing public incidents, like the time I knocked down ninety percent of the canned foods aisle. It wasn't my fault. Desperate and under immense pressure, I climbed the store shelves to fetch the last can of green beans from the back needed for a green bean casserole. I wanted to impress Hank with my cheap culinary skills.

"Molly, have you considered volunteering? It would do you some good to get out of the house," Walter chimed in with his opinion, knowing his comment completely annoyed me.

"I get out of the house plenty. And I'm too busy keeping this place clean." I glanced around at the dust and dog hair covered furniture, and then at the laundry pile taking up permanent residency on the mud room floor. Okay, maybe I did fall a little behind on my chores.

"You should listen to Walt," Hank agreed.

No doubt my flawless husband was right. I could do something useful like stay home and clean the house. Start a hobby, or join a book discussion group, except that would require actually reading the book. I could volunteer at an old folk's home. No, scratch that idea. Volunteers don't get paid. I'm sure somewhere on the mainland there are plenty of opportunities to become a noble, dutiful person. It's just that I'd rather have an appendectomy performed without anesthesia. All I really want is to solve puzzles. Not the stupid puzzle book kind found in office waiting rooms or next to the toilet, but those of comic book caped crusaders and television detectives. They always bust the bad guys and save the day in the end. My desire to be the hero originated when I was a kid playing in the yard slaying invisible dragons and boogie men and that yearning is just as strong in my adulthood.

"What would you think if I became a Private Investigator? I think I'd be good at it. I could put my talents and skills to use instead of wasting them on the island tending the crab house."

Hank's immediate knee-jerk reaction was to say nothing, and neither did his jerk-face friend, Walter. Instead, they both completely ignored my suggestions. This was going nowhere fast. I sat up, straightening my posture from a slump, "Then how about a job at Walmart?" I knew this would get their back hairs standing upright.

"No," Hank and Walter shouted in unison.

"I could work security, be a guard in uniform with a spiffy shoulder patch and take down shoplifters. I would save the store millions in petty theft. Come to think of it, the security job is very similar to PI work. I bet there's a course I could take up at Somerville University," I said, excited at the prospect of having a respectable job, then I would become cool again.

"No," said Hank firmly.

"But you know how brilliant I'd be in that line of work." I turned to Walter, "It's true."

"No," he reiterated, violently shaking his head. "Chances are you'd end up tangled in a dangerous mess, hurt, or arrested.

"Okay, okay I get it. I'll look into employment elsewhere then," I said, knowing that I wouldn't.

"Maybe you should stick to tinkering with that glass sculpture hobby of yours."

"They are works of art that just so happen to add to my income and self-worth. In fact, I am in the process of creating several pieces for a gallery in Virginia. Who knows where it will lead." In reality the income is quite small, and wouldn't be worth mentioning if he hadn't sounded so condescending.

"Before you run off with a head full of big ideas, I think you should look into taking a few courses over at the community college first. I hear the forensics course will be starting up in the new criminal justice department wing," Hank mentioned, picking up on my indignation.

"He's right Molly; it's a professional lab often used by authorities as a hands-on teaching course. We're talking real high tech." By the time Walter pitched his two cents that landed nowhere, it was too late.

"It would suit you," Hank added.

"I know that," I said in an indignant manner. "I'll check out the college tomorrow online. Anything I can do to help with dinner?" I offered, but Hank already had set the table. Timing was everything.

"No, but thank you." Hank shut the gas stove off, pulled several serving platters from the cabinet, and began dishing out the food. He placed a massive bowl of mashed potatoes on the table, followed by a platter of deer meat he shot last month during firearm season, which I would pass on. I gave up eating meat years ago, not for political reasons, but in fear of waking up one day reincarnated as a chicken neatly wrapped in plastic in the grocery store meat aisle. There are instances when the scent of the Gas & Go Mart's all beef jumbo hotdog twirling on a rotisserie behind protective glass brings a salivating memory of greasy hot monosodium glutamate dripping down my chin that could make me fall off the meat wagon.

Preoccupied by my strange run-in earlier today at the Gas & Go Mart, their conversational din swam in my ears. There was no time like the present to hit up Walter.

"Hey, Walt, what can you tell me about those recent Amber Alert messages, the ones on the teenage girls?"

"Molly, you know more than anyone that I can't say anything to you. Official police business automatically places restraints on all information pertaining to the case, it's to protect the victims.

So, you think the victims are connected?"

"No, I didn't say that."

"Then tell me this, Walt. How come I can find out more about current events just by listening to the local news station, than I can from you? Two Amber Alerts in one week, and now a third girl is missing. I thought you were privy to police business. I guess you're not as important as I thought."

"Molly, you have no problem with getting to the point, do you?" Walter responded annoyed.

"I don't see a point in wasting time."

"Not when it comes to your tenacity, I suppose there isn't."

"Now you're being reasonable. I like this side of you, Walt."

"Don't get used to it."

"It's refreshing seeing you both getting along for once," said Hank.

"Thanks buddy, you know I'm not the one who's the problem here. All the bullshit trouble Molly causes could fill the black hole in outer space."

"Don't get your man panties in a twist, Walter." I couldn't help myself.

"Ease up Walt, do it for me before you blow my dinner plans to smithereens."

"You're right, Hank. I'll tell her what's already public knowledge, but that's all, and I mean it."

"That would be very congenial on your part. Dinner's ready. Hope you two are hungry."

Walter moved his chair closer to the table, filling his plate high. "This all looks wonderful. Thanks again for the invite, Hank. I can't remember when I had a home cooked meal last. You are one lucky woman, Molly. A good man is hard to find, and so is a good woman. I should know, I had one."

Hank gave me a furtive glance which I acknowledged with a raised eyebrow.

Walter's wife, Linda, died three years ago after a second bout of breast cancer. Lately, he'd been opening up with loving stories about his wife, far from his usual tight-as-a-clam's ass demeanor. Navigating life alone now, Walter's weight had snuck up on him, clocked him over the head, and drug him off to every fast-food drive-through in town.

Linda was a special, sweet person, and the love of Walter's life, a love he pines for every day. Tonight, for some strange reason, I had been stricken by a sudden compassion towards Walter. I hate when that happens. Seeing a big burly man become emotionally overwhelmed when speaking about his dead wife, makes me very uncomfortable. It upsets the balance in our relationship. I know I should show compassion, and try not to harangue him about his weight as often as I normally do. Problem being, my personality doesn't allow for that kind of emotional response. Besides, when it comes to Walter, I like poking the fat bear with a big stick.

An awkwardness enveloped the room, suffocating us all. For everyone's sake, I broke the silence. "Well, Sherriff Big Man, are you going to tell me what the department knows, or what?"

"Molly, a little tact can go a long way," Hank remarked, miffed.

Walter cleared his throat, "It's alright Hank. I know she's itching to hear something juicy. I know a few things that may spark her interest." Before proceeding, Walter raked a hand through his thinning hair and chewed the inside of his cheek pondering the safest way to respond.

"Go on," I said, leaning forward in the chair.

"The authorities feel there may be a connection to the latest girl missing from Fairview. She was reported missing by her grandmother a few days ago. She never came home from school. You know, I shouldn't be talking about this, it's confidential official business and all," said Walter, and that was enough to set my ears burning.

Fairview is the first mainland town after the marsh. It's unsettling to hear a girl's missing this close to home.

"My lips are sealed shut. I promise not to repeat this to anyone," I said, thinking there's no guarantee I won't act on it.

"I heard she never made it home from school," added Hank, and passed the food around for a second helping after plopping extra potatoes on his plate smothered in gravy.

"Was the granddaughter skinny, with long blondish hair?" I asked Walter, as he handed over the almost empty bowl of potatoes. I shot him a look.

"Nope, haven't heard about that one. Mind you, the increase in missing reports certainly is cause for alarm," he answered, shoveling the last of the potatoes in his mouth.

"I picked up a young blonde girl hitching a ride from the Gas & Go Mart. I saw her come out from that hokey house across the street. You know the one, Walt, the house with all the junk cars in the yards that's by your office. What's going on over there anyway?"

"I'm not sure what you mean."

"I saw the girl in a heated argument with the owner of that weird house when she jumped out of his station wagon. He went after her shouting and making a big scene loud enough for everyone at the Gas & Go Mart to hear. Then the man took off and left her there standing in the lot."

"Sounds to me like the average couple having a spat."

"No, this was different. The frantic girl went from car to car asking for money."

"Wait a second, tell me you didn't pick up a hitchhiker. Molly, that's dangerous, not to mention stupid. I don't want you picking up strange people. What are you thinking? This is just dandy, you gave me another reason to fret, thanks a lot," Hank's voice snapped, becoming more irritated with each word. It didn't bother me. I'm used to it.

"You didn't see how frightened the girl was by that oddball. You must have seen him, Walt, dressed in army fatigues, even in the summer when it's a hundred degrees outside. His place looks like a junk yard. Every time I drive by that house, I see a new hunk of metal trash sprouting in the yard. The side of the house was left wide open for months, then haphazardly boarded over. Now it looks like crap. It's the first thing people see when driving by the *Welcome to Somerset County* billboard. I'm surprised the county hadn't penalized the owner for letting the weeds grow so tall. Maybe the guy was trying to hide his ugly house behind all the weeds and the trash. Who can live like that? Something ain't right about him, that's for sure. What's your department doing about that eyesore Walt?" I demanded, but didn't receive a reply. Judging by their stunned faces, I thought it was too much information to digest on a full stomach, and waited for clarity to return.

"Didn't you think the camouflage is necessary because he's serving in the National Guard, or another type of armed forces?" Walter asked, trying to steer me off the subject, but I wasn't falling for it, nor would I let it go.

"Militia seems more like it. I bet he's a doomsday-prepper and has an underground bunker stockpiled with various artillery and dehydrated foods lining the shelves."

"He's a what?" Hank jumped in the conversation.

"You know, people who collect food products, batteries and guns, readying for Armageddon. The guy fits the profile." Envisioning the man's house packed floor to ceiling with assault rifles was easy. My mind ticked like an antique Grandfather's Clock at the sides of my temple. My Gas & Go Mart experience did not leave me with a warm and fuzzy upstanding feeling about Camo Man. With the way he behaved, I had every reason to doubt his motives.

"Listen up, Walt, Molly happens to be making sense. Last week I was stuck behind a garbage truck and noticed two high school girls exit the front seat of the vehicle and go inside that house. And get this, I saw the weird guy standing on the porch like he was expecting their arrival. And it was during school hours," Hank said, reassuringly touching the back of my hand. I looked up and smiled.

"The man hasn't broken any laws. You're blowing this out of proportion, just like Molly."

"Okay, this has been fun, but that's enough of this nonsense. We should change the subject." Hank got up from the table and spoke through a yawn, "That was a fantastic dinner even if I say so myself."

"Agreed," said Walter, stretching in synchronized movements.

Hank's second yawn was our cue to end the evening. Walter recited his appreciation for the hospitality and the meal, then he left for home. I started cleaning up the mess in the kitchen. To my surprise, Hank stayed behind in the room while I cleared the dishes.

"What's your opinion on finding Walt a girlfriend?" I asked.

"I think you should forget it, Molly. Wandering into other people's business backfires every time."

"Don't you think Walter's grieved long enough? It wouldn't hurt to put himself out there in the dating scene again."

"That's Walt's decision to make, not yours."

"I'm just saying, that's all."

"Never mind that. We're alone now. You can say what's really bugging you, and don't say it's nothing because I can tell when you got something stuck in your craw."

"What do you mean? I'm fine," I lied again.

"You were distant most of the evening, and that's not like you. If I upset you earlier, I'm sorry. I overreacted about the hitchhiker, but you can't blame me for blowing a gasket."

"No, it's alright. I just have a lot on my mind. I'll be fine really, I will." I stopped washing the dishes, turned off the water, and turned to look at my husband. Hank's demeanor was fraught with concern. How can I tell him what's wrong when I didn't even know myself, other than I'm fed up with my sister, and hadn't a clue how to file my mother's death into normalcy, and how the Amber Alerts are beginning to unravel my nerves. What bothers me the most is the worry my shenanigans cause my husband. If only I could mind my own business. I grazed the palm of my hand along the side of Hank's face. "Can I ask you to do something for me?"

"Of course, anything," replied Hank, his eyebrows narrowed in apprehension.

"If I die before you, I don't want you to waste your life grieving like Walt. No longer than two weeks, tops," I stated, as if it were law, then resumed cleaning the dishes.

"So, now you're going to boss me around after you're dead?" Hank stiffened in protest.

"You need to return to your life as soon as possible. I know how you are. You'll go mad standing in one place."

The corner of Hank's mouth formed a flirtatious smile, one that has the power to make me want to do bad things. He tugged me in close, breathing warm words into my neck. Goosebumps traveled to body parts that made me grateful to God for making me a woman.

"Oh sweetheart, you worry too much about nothing," he said.

"That's just it. I want you to be happy. I want things to stay normal." I held him tighter, inhaling his scent.

Hank softly laughed, "Molly, my life left behind normal the very moment we met, and I wouldn't change that for the world."

- six -

"Damn it," I winced as warm blood trickled down my finger forming red droplets on the floor, something I've become accustomed to when sifting broken pieces of glass collected from Piney Island. I sliced my finger on a busted piece of brown beer glass. Luckily, it was not my middle finger or I wouldn't be able to drive.

The type of broken glass I normally discover originates from the once inhabited island beaches, a minimum one-hundred years in age. Older glass pieces tend to be colored in frosted pastels after tossing for centuries in the salty water. The offending piece of glass that cut my finger however, was from circa right-now, and the only tossing it ever received was from a weekend tourist over the gunnel of his crass speedboat. Hank doesn't hold back opinions when it comes to the weekend warriors who tear up the commercial fishing waters and cut buoy lines. He refers to them in perfect diction as *Googins*. Idiots that run through designated fishing areas at high speeds, smashing crab pots into unrecognizable and unusable forms. Losing crab pots to the Tangier Sound's bottom adds a costly sum to the watermen's bottom line. This riles Hank to the point of no return. One of these days I fear he may go off the deep end and ram his Southern Skimmer boat right through the middle of a *Googin's* vessel.

The locals also have coined a title fit for all outsiders who relocate to the island. They're called *Come Here*. I have, and will forever be, referred to as a *Come Here* until my dying day. Though friendly to an extent, the islanders view a *Come Here* with suspicion that inevitably becomes a threat to island tradition. Any ill occurrence, locally or globally, is blamed on the *Come Here*.

After all these years, I'm still not comfortable with island living, and may never be. I'm caught in limbo, existing somewhere between belonging and a *Come Here*. I think I would prefer island living a whole lot more if the inhabitants were just me, my husband, and the dogs, and maybe a small sized Walmart within walking distance.

Barring my existence, Smithtown had remained unchanged since the community was moved across the water from Piney Island one hundred and twenty-five years ago, after saltwater claimed the land. Five of the original homes are still standing strong, including our drafty dwelling. I have become accustomed to the mucky odors of life decomposing at the water's bottom. And I've grown quite fond of the colors of the marsh and all the life it brings forth. If island life wasn't so challenging every waking moment, then I wouldn't mind calling it home.

Although its people, with their skiffs and stern-wheelers have long since departed the island, proof of their once thriving existence remains behind in trash that I turn into upmarket treasure. Recently, I've been focusing on nighttime art illuminated by tiny white Christmas lights. The glass sculptures are decorative in the day, or night, and the collection process rids the beaches of trash. Fortunately, the sculptures appeal to the tourists who don't mind overpaying for assembled refuse. The creations save my dignity from becoming reduced to a fish wife as my lot in life.

My cell phone buzzed in my pocket. The caller readout said Megan in all caps. I reluctantly answered, "Psychic hotline, how may I help you?"

"Hi. It's me, your sister calling," she said, with dramatic pauses separating her words. "Are you busy?"

"Not since I moved to the island, what's up?" I asked, searching my mind for a legitimate reason to ring off.

"I don't mean to be a burden, but I don't know how to begin to unload all these feelings bottled up inside of me. You're the only person who understands how I feel. I'm sorry. I know I'm a pest. You have always been so good to me, even when I treated you badly as kids."

"You are not a pest." No, not a pest, but certainly an expert in laying on a guilt trip with ease. This call was heading down a road I am more than exhausted traveling. Everyone in the world has had to deal with some sort of raging storm in their life. Megan has been a full-blown category five hurricane, wearing her battle scars like a war medal. I've done my best to move on. I don't need any of her five-and-dime store philosophy.

The most disappointing consensus in the way I conduct my life, is that I could care less about what other people think, and even less about their problems.

"Are you still there?" I asked Megan. I once again braced myself for the talk. "Tell me what could be the problem now?"

"I can't stop crying. I just miss them so much. I have this horrible hollow feeling that I will never see them again." Megan sobbed into the phone, choking on her tears. I suppose it was wrong to act insensitive, just a knee jerk reaction on my part. I don't understand her willingness to dredge up our turbulent history again and again, grinding it to a sticky mental paste. She was hurting, and I would fix this, just like I did many occasions before.

"Listen, I understand how you feel and how much you miss them. Try closing your eyes and remember all the wonderful things about them. Love has more power than anything else in this world. They loved you with all their hearts and that will never go away," I explained. This is what you say with conviction to bereaved persons as if it were fact. The thing is, I so wanted it to be true.

"How can you be so sure?" she sniffled into the receiver.

"I can't explain it, I just know."

"Did you find God, or something?"

"Yes, something like that. It wasn't looking, but he found me anyway. All I know is that I believe."

"Believe in what? Some happy ever after-life bouncing around on puffy clouds in white robes playing harps? You can't be serious." Megan turned somber, with a touch of snarky. Probably put off because I had something she didn't. Some things never change.

"All I'm saying is I believe in a God and all that other holy stuff."

"I struggle with that concept." Megan's voice wavered again, now laden with grief that left her wrung out like an old dish rag.

"It's easy. Choose God and he will choose you." Religion happens as a matter of course after several near-death experiences. It's a holy miracle I'm still walking on this planet.

"I appreciate what you're saying, but I'm not sure it helps. I miss them so much that sometimes it feels like I can't breathe."

"Listen to me Megan, holding onto mom's clothing will not keep her spirit alive. It's what you hold in your heart that keeps her close. Try and remember the joy, not her death." If I were able to make Megan understand death was the temporary passing of the physical life, I would have by now.

"I try but it's so hard."

"Do you remember the fun we had when we were young? Like before dad had finished off the second bedroom and we were stuck sharing a bed for years," I asked, stopping there. It was not the right moment to bring up my sister's nightly smothering performance.

"Dad was talented in so many ways, wasn't he? He could fix anything, cars, TVs or appliances, except for that toaster."

"Yes, the one that gave off a small electrical shock when you touched the lever," I added, and Megan chuckled a little. "Do you remember me pushing you out of bed and landing hard on the floor loud enough to wake our parents?" I asked.

"And how about when I held a pillow over your face," she laughed, and I wondered how on earth could she think that was funny.

"Remember the time you ran away and nobody noticed?" I fired in defense and the laughter grew between us, familiar and natural, the way we once were. I began to wonder if it truly was impossible to rekindle our relationship after all these years.

"Do you remember the soap we had that grew hair?" I asked. Lacking as I am in the compassion department, I'm lucky to have humor readily available to make up for it.

"Yep. Fuzzy Wuzzy the Bear soaps." Megan confirmed my memory's reliability.

"No wonder New Jersey had the highest cancer rate. Now I know why Jersey girls' glow in the dark." I sensed my sister would be fine. They say laughter cures all ills. I prefer wine to heal me.

"Wouldn't it be wonderful if we could laugh like this all the time?"

"Megan, I want you to remember something."

"What's that?"

"You're never alone. You have me, and our parents. They're always with you in your memories and in your heart."

"You mean like a guardian angel?" Megan pondered the possibility.

"Yeah, something like that."

"Do you have an angel?"

"Yes, I do, but I think my angel may have a drinking problem," I smirked.

"Thanks Molly. You always know how to make me feel better."

I disconnected the call with a surprising sentiment towards my sister, more than I care to admit. It's not my style. How on earth am I supposed to help her, when I'm having enough trouble fitting into my own hot mess? Lord knows I need the hand up as much as Megan, though I would never ask her, or anyone for help, including God for that matter. I see badgering God with trivial requests to be in poor taste.

Last summer, during a persistent heat wave that peaked mid-July, the van's driver side window quit working, and shortly after, so did the air conditioning mechanisms. I was driving north in a sweltering vehicle and had to stop for the red light at the Somerville intersection. Waiting for the light to turn green, I noticed a mobile baptism trailer unit parked to the right of the road near Mickey D's. The trailer was painted white and large in size, similar to caravans used by a traveling circus. I debated whether or not I should pop in for a quick churching-up until the stoplight changed to green. Being miserable from the extreme heat, I kept on driving. Judging by the shouts emanating from the unit, they were using live snakes, and I regret to this day not going inside to see for myself. In many ways, I view God as being like a *Genie in a Bottle* who grants a limited number of prayer requests. I'm careful to use my prayers sparingly for those who sincerely are in need. I'm just not that certain my sister is deserving of one.

- seven -

Sara Jane whined at the back door, wanting outside. Turning the knob, I was immediately greeted by a glacial slap to the face announcing that winter had officially arrived. The temperature had fallen drastically overnight and transformed the morning air to a bitter and difficult task to breathe. Waking up in a cold antique shore house serves to remind me how much I hate the winters on the island, and the dreadful unforgiving winds. It's the kind of cold that burns to the bone and will dry out skin to crack and bleed. The winter months force me indoors for the entire duration, like a caterpillar in a cocoon waiting to emerge in the spring completely renewed by the warming sun.

On the water, I saw white-caps freeze mid-air and thought how ridiculous the sight was. Island weather is dangerously unpredictable year-round. I dreaded the drive ahead of me in temperatures determined to burn my bones. But I was on a deadline and had to deliver my artwork to the gallery by the end of the day. I was flat broke. Hopefully, the holiday shopping rush would yield the much-needed sales, and hamper Hank's persistent hounding about my seeking viable employment. It's not like I didn't try and find work.

Okay, maybe I haven't given it my best shot. I work hard keeping house, and cleaning the crab house. I find it ironic that the world believes the seafood industry operates by the sweat on a watermen's back, but in reality, it's the women who run the show. Tending the crab house is disgusting, tedious labor conducted in brutal humid summer heat. It is monotonous busy work that stifles all imagination. Winter is the extreme opposite, and incredibly boring. When I become bored, my hamster wheel starts to spin with adventures that inevitably equals trouble and an irritated husband who says I need to find a real job. It's a vicious cycle. If sculpture sales don't pan out soon, I'll have to figure out something else before Hank pushes for me to find a crappy minimum wage job flipping burgers. The perfect career move for me would have to be solving crimes and saving humanity from certain doom. Several times I had searched employment opportunities online, but failed to find a superhero opening in the classifieds.

The gale struck the house with a fervent force, stressing the foundation boards to moan. Cold winds would have formed sporadic patches of ice on the roads. The sketchy drive will be even more miserable with a reluctant car heater. Despite the condition of my vehicle, the engine purrs like an overfed cat with two hundred and fifty-four thousand miles on the odometer. Even though body parts fall off at random, and air is beginning to show through the floorboards, I'm confident the van will top three hundred thousand miles with no problem.

Before leaving the house, I left a note for Hank on the kitchen table, and then set the coffee pot on a timer for his return. Regardless of the number of bad habits I maintain, I also manage a few favorable traits. Preparing Hank's coffee was the one nice thing I do consistently for my husband. Everything else like dressing tastefully, or behaving appropriately is ignored. Hank says I have a bad case of Peter Pan Syndrome, and spend too much time in my head with my imaginary friends. He thinks I push the shenanigan envelope to the verge of breaking. I love my husband deeply, but his motivation to marry me was the eighth wonder of the world.

The weather sustained its assault on the house, hurling tree branches and pinecones, denting the aluminum siding. The one redeeming factor about island winters, are the cooler temperatures that bring reprieve from the sticky hot summer and the throngs of insects that drive Smithtown residents to profanity with each maddening bite. In the entire calendar year, enjoyable days are limited to about two weeks at best.

Readying myself for the elements, I dressed in as many layers of clothing as would fit under my heavy coat, then began loading my junk-glass light sculptures, carefully securing the boxes for the ride. I checked the time, noting the whole morning had flown by without one Amber Alert, or a stupid phone call from Megan. I put the car in gear and left the downtown metropolis of Smithtown Island freezing my ass off with a renewed hope of escaping the troubling aspect of my world. And I just might make a couple of bucks to boot.

- eight -

Out on highway route thirteen, the southbound lanes were exceedingly congested and I had to use extra caution merging the van into the traffic. In the fast lane to my left, cars blurred past well over the speed limit. Behind me, the driver of a black SUV hugged my bumper, and found it necessary to lay on the car horn.

"Gee whiz, lighten up buddy. It's a minivan for Pete's sake," I shouted as if he could hear me and then flipped him the bird just in case he didn't. I refused to let his road rage rattle my nerves and turned my attention to the sun flickering between the buildings in a seizure-inducing strobe light effect.

I pulled the visor down and punched the dashboard with a hopeful fist, coaxing the heater to work. It finally kicked in, hissing a slightly warmer air through the vents, returning sensation to my toes. I settled in for the long drive thinking about the holiday. With any luck, the shopping frenzy would spill over into the gallery and my light box sculptures would sell out.

Several cars behind, I caught a flash of red lights in my rearview. Two brand new shiny sheriff department's cars whooshed by at high speeds, rocking the van as they passed. The sheriff's department recently replaced all the squad's vehicles with state-of-the-art cruisers, outfitted with roof mounted tag readers, grille collision guards, rolling LED lights, tinted glass, high-tech laptops, and a Bluetooth printer within the headrest. Walter opted for his older model, a gas guzzling Grand Vic with an old-fashioned bubble light, because the bench seats were comfortable on his back after years of molding perfectly around his expanding form.

During each shift, there's a minimum of three deputy sheriff officers patrolling throughout the far corners of the county twenty-four-seven, with each cruiser strategically placed within immediate response time to the other. They swim the highways and backroads like a pool of sharks, alert and waiting for the call to respond. Walter's more than willing to assist the other officers in need, but at this stage in the game, he's usually not the first to respond unless the incident happens to occur near a fast-food joint.

Maybe I'll stop by his office on the way home. He might be a little more forthcoming without Hank in the room.

I switched the radio on to a familiar country station, sang along off key, a genetic trait I inherited from my mother's side. Being completely tone-deaf never slowed her enjoyment in belting out a tune whenever the urge struck.

The traffic calmed somewhat, maintaining a steady roll. Further up, on the right side of the highway, I saw someone walking close to the shoulder line, causing several cars to swerve. Squinting at the form, I realized the person was thumbing a ride and heard Hank's voice inside my head. *Don't do it Molly. Don't ever pick up hitchhikers. There are too many nut bags out there now. Stranger Means Danger. You'll end up deader than a rusted door nail, hacked to pieces and thrown in a dumpster.*

"Don't do it," I said out loud, and powered on past, seeing the hitcher grow smaller in the mirror. It stirred a familiar scene of the Gas & Go Mart girl's fading image to tug at my better judgment. The weather was cruel and incredibly cold. He wouldn't be able to endure these temperatures for very long. A rush of guilt ran through me. I needed to quit complaining about the van's heater, my cold house, and life in general as well.

Driving a couple hundred yards past the hitchhiker, I found a safe place to pull the van off the road. The man's attention remained on the mass of cars. I signaled him with the car horn then watched as he gathered his tan duffel-bag and heaved a backpack over his shoulder, running scary scenarios through my mind. Each outcome showed my life ending in a bloody gory death. My intestines stirred nervously as the man struggled under his heavy belongings. He wore a tan canvas coat and army issued cargo pants. The man didn't look like a serial killer, but then again, I'm not sure what serial killers are supposed to look like.

As he approached the van, I slid my wallet under the driver seat, unsure of the importance of hiding an empty wallet. The chances of picking up a random serial killer on a busy highway were probably not in my favor. I reached out and opened the side door, then waited like a dumbass sitting duck. This had to be the stupidest thing I have ever done. Okay, perhaps not the stupidest.

There are a gazillion reasons why I should forget helping this guy and take off right now. That would be the smarter course, but all sensibility had flown right out the window instead. If he tries anything funny, I'll simply run the van off the road, splattering us both on the spot.

"Hello, I have ID," said the cherry red face. The man drew his wallet. "My name's Christopher, see? Thank you for stopping. I've been out here a long while." The man presented a plastic photo identification card.

"Un-huh, I have an ID in my wallet as well. I could show you, but it's under the seat," I answered prematurely before I could think straight. I can't believe I told him where my wallet was. I'm such a duh-head. "Throw your stuff in the back, there's plenty of room."

The hitchhiker surveyed the van packed to the gills with boxes that left very little space for his worldly goods. He plopped the bag down on the only vacant spot behind the seats, then pulled the door closed. Each movement he made was slow, apprehensive, appearing more nervous about climbing in the van than I was about letting him inside.

"Here's my ID," he flashed his wallet again.

"Thanks, my name's Molly," I replied, straining at the fine print on the plastic card, pretending to read the small letters without my reading glasses I left sitting on the kitchen table. For all I knew it was a stolen library card.

"Does it say your last name is Nicholas?" I asked, sensing my eyes were about to fall out of their sockets from the strain. "Isn't that normally a first name?"

"It can be, but not in my case. Thanks again for picking me up." He settled in for the ride, rubbing his hands, jump-starting his circulation.

"This sudden cold snap's crazy. It's too bitter out there for hitching rides," I said, shifting the van into gear, then eased into the manic traffic lanes. "I'm heading to Onancock, Virginia. How far down are you going?"

"Tennessee," he replied, still rubbing his hands together. "I have to make it there by tomorrow. Then I'm heading up north for a big job that needs my attention.

"I'm sorry about the heater. This is as warm as it gets." I slammed my fist on the dashboard once more with optimism, hoping the infernal heater would rise to the challenge.

"Compared to last night, I think the temperature is nice and toasty. I can't tell you how grateful I am. I was beginning to worry no one would give me a lift. People don't stop for hitchhikers like they used to. The media's paranoia has got everyone spooked. It's a different kind of world we live in now."

"Thumbing a ride in these conditions must be unbearable. Have you considered catching a lift with a trucker? Don't they usually travel across the state lines, heading to every destination on the map?"

"You're right about that, they run nonstop. Truckers face huge fines for picking up people on a highway. I stay in congested traffic areas, it's easier to snag a ride.

"Isn't picking up hitchhikers illegal for everyone?" *Not to mention stupid.*

"No, it's not illegal, but it is prohibited on certain roads like highways. Could be risky on any road."

Gee, why didn't I think of that? "What about a truck stop, can't you sneak a ride there? You'll catch pneumonia in this weather,"

I repeated like it mattered to him. Serial Killers work in all sorts of weather.

"Once and a while I hop on a big rig and cover ground nonstop. I hope to hook up with a trucker down by the fifteen-mile bridge. The last person to pick me up was a woman. She had her young son with her in the car. Real nice people, they were."

My mind reeled. What if he killed them both and left their bodies in the car to rot? It's good to know I'm not the only soft-headed woman out here picking up strangers. Best to schmooze his good side and steer the man far from any murderous ideas.

"You mentioned Tennessee, that's a long way off from here," I noted, while fretting about dead bodies.

He grunted like it wasn't his favorite subject.

Convincing the hitcher that I was a nice person, the sweet motherly type, meant maybe he wouldn't kill me, though most serial murderers have issues about their mothers. I had gathered this information by watching a documentary about convicted serial murderer, Edward Gains, and it gave me the willies. This nut-bag earned his claim-to-fame from skinning human corpses, a similar process to what hunters perform when removing a deer hide, only Eddy created a human bodysuit and pretended to be his dead mother. This grisly and heinous act became the source of inspiration for the film *Psycho*, and as a result millions of people now shower with the curtain partially open. I should have recalled this little tidbit of information before I let this guy in my van.

"I went to college in Tennessee for business. It's hard to get anywhere in this economy, let alone without a degree. Tuition pricing has skyrocketed, and so has campus housing. Colleges are an unregulated business that care only about money. Kids drowning in student debt before the first day of class, dropping out halfway through their academic year because they can't afford it. Or stick with it and can't even get a decent job to repay their student loans. I'm not one for big brother governments, but I think in this situation the system is past due and needs to step in and do something about the cost of tuition."

I was completely taken back by the serial killer's educated air about him. He was certainly knowledgeable. I was ashamed of myself for assuming he wasn't.

The man continued rambling, switching to interest and mortgage rates. He took note of all the depressed areas as we passed by the once stately homes.

"I can remember when these houses were alive with families," he said. "Now look at them. Abandoned souls left to decay. Such a waste to see with so many homeless people needing a place to call their own."

As he reminisced about life as it once was, I periodically snuck a glance at his face. The man seemed familiar, like someone I may have known before. He was a bit overweight, soft and rounded at the edges. His mannerisms were tender, and his thoughts worldly and not like the typical Somerset County druggies more commonly seen hitching on highways.

"Are you from around here? You sound like you know a lot about the area," I asked, finally letting go of his role as a serial killer.

"Yeppers, I grew up in Crisfield. Started working on a commercial fishing boat right after high school graduation, pulling crab pots in the summer. Boy oh boy, that sure was hard work. I dated a girl from the town of Sandpoint. She came from a family of hard-working watermen. The whole town was made up of fishermen." As he smiled, his face glazed over in sweet memory. "We were considering marriage, but my job is based way up north, and she preferred a warmer climate."

I sneaked another peek at the guy. By his outward appearance, he looked to be climbing the ranks of the unemployed.

"Crisfield you say? My husband and I live not far from there in Smithtown, do you know where that is?"

What is wrong with me? I must be giddy from being nervous. Perhaps it was stupid to reveal my location, but this offbeat person riding in my car was easy to talk to, like an old friend, allowing my personal information to glide like oil over a puddle.

"Yes, I know Smithtown. Not much happens out there."

"You got that right. It's deader than roadkill on the highway. We live in a smaller shore home originally built on Piney Island, long ago when the island was a thriving community."

"Oh, I know all about its history moving all those houses off the island when the saltwater encroached the land and made it inhabitable. Are you renovating the house?" he asked.

I noticed his skin tone adjusted from a pale-purple, to flush-red as his circulation returned.

"We're trying to renovate, but the work is more focused on repairing. We still have damage to fix from when Hurricane Sandy hit. It's an awful cold house, with the temperature rising to a balmy fifty-five degrees on a sunny winter day. It's similar to one of those over there, old and frigid," I pointed towards a house set at the far end of the field that had turned brown.

"Ah, yes, Sandy. Some say it wouldn't have been as bad if not for that king-tide."

I was familiar with what kind of damage a king-tide can bring on the island. Once a year, the tide rolls around the world, bringing high water to the eastern communities. In 2012, the damaging king-tide occurred simultaneously with deadly forces from Hurricane Sandy and destroyed the northeastern shoreline homes. Its hardest strike smashed the New Jersey coastline.

Hurricane Sandy was the highest recorded water in Tangier Sound's history. The majority of coastal watermen towns are only a few feet above sea level. The hurricane flooded the towns terribly for weeks until the water finally receded to a normal tidal rhythm.

Over in the fishing town of Porter, on the lowest part of their water table, stands a historical Protestant church where worship services are still conducted regularly on Sunday mornings. The combination of a king-tide and a hurricane put a great strain on the church graveyard shifting the caskets in the waterlogged ground. The road department came to the rescue by moving the wayward caskets back to their rightful resting places.

The most recent king-tide crept into Smithtown without force or fanfare, catching even the veteran residents off guard. It rolled under our house, soaking the ductwork, and upset the plastic recycle bin. Empty wine bottles bobbed around the backyard for days.

"Do you happen to know what the temperatures went down to last night?" he asked. "Was it bad on the island?"

When he turned his crimson face from the road towards me for a brief second, I caught a glimpse of his steely blue eyes sparkling in three dimensions. Suspended by their power, it felt as if this hitch hiker man knew my every wish, everything I desired. We must have met somewhere before, once when I was young. Yes, that's it, I'm sure I went to school with him.

But that couldn't be, he's much younger than me now. He was a good ten to fifteen-years older when he first climbed into the van. But that's crazy. It must be the car heater resurrecting him back to life.

"Are you alright? You seem like you've seen a ghost," he asked.

No, it wasn't a ghost, but I was certain I saw something.

"I'm fine, just the glare from the sun," I replied, searching his eyes for that sparkle, but they had returned to normal shade of blue.

"Are those Amber Alerts making you jumpy?" he asked with a raised eyebrow.

"Wait, how did you know?"

"I received three Amber Alert texts on my phone, which I thought was a lot for a small town like Somerville."

"I agree, but I don't understand why you're receiving text from our area." This was getting weirder by the second. I never should have let this guy in my car. My hands gripped the wheel tighter, my knuckles turned a translucent white.

"I kept my old number and still receive local Amber Alerts. I also get a boat load of spam and robo calls. Traveling as much as I do, a cell phone's about as essential as thermal socks."

"That would make sense." I said, letting out a sigh of relief, realizing that all this fear manifesting in my head was the product of an overactive imagination. I was not facing imminent death inviting this ride-along companion into my car. "To answer your question, yes, it was freezing last night. Heavy winds ripped across the island, pelting pinecones at the side of the house until dawn. I barely slept a wink for the racket."

"I found a spot to hunker down out of the wind. You're correct about last night, it was a cold one alright. My trusty sleeping bag did the trick. Come the morning I was happy to see my feet were still pink. I wasn't wearing socks. I got them wet earlier in the day and had to dry them by morning," he looked down at his feet, as if relieved they were still there. "I sure wish spring would make a decision and stay around for good. I'll be a lot warmer in Tennessee."

The idea of any human being sleeping outside in that kind of weather was awful. I sound like a prize idiot whining about my house. I should be grateful to have food, heat, and a safe place to sleep every night. We had an extra bed and a couch he could have slept on. If Hank knew about his situation, he would have fixed up the guest room, bought him new clothes, and fed him like a king. I would have slept with one eye open. I'm not as good and trusting as my husband.

"Did you mention where you were traveling from?" I asked, but I knew with the amount of heavy weather gear the man was hauling, it wasn't from someplace warm.

"I started out up north, above Canada. It's harder hitching a ride the further south I go."

"Is that because there's so much land between towns?"

"No, that's not it. Southerners just ain't as trusting."

The vision of the little round man hiking along the murky roads by endless fields, with no hope of seeing headlights popped into my head. Even if he did come across a car, chances were that they wouldn't stop to pick him up. My previous fear of being murdered by this transient person transmuted into deep concern for his well-being.

"Are you warm enough? I'm sorry about the heater," I asked once again.

"I'm good thanks," he smiled. "We're almost to the Virginia line. There's a big town coming up soon."

"Yes, I would be turning off at the stoplight, but I could keep on driving and take you to the bridge if you'd like. There's a truck stop there." I asked, slowing the van.

"No, it's alright. I'll get a ride at the light."

"There's a convenience store gas station on the corner. They make decent sandwiches, and it's warm inside. How bout I buy you lunch?"

Heavily focused on scanning the area, the man didn't reply to my offer. "Drop me off at the light. Visibility is key when hitching rides," he said, the stress in his voice markedly rising.

"But it's so cold out."

"That it is."

I pulled onto the side of the road, shifted into park, and let the engine run to keep warm.

As he gauged the traffic, I saw his character morph into survival mode. "Thanks, this is perfect," he said, darting to the rear of the van to collect his belongings.

I felt overwhelmed by an urge to protect him, take him home and feed him.

"Thanks again for the ride and lunch offer, but I have to keep moving. You be careful out there. Lots of wackos on the road," he smiled, giving a wink and a two-finger wave from his brow. With a heavy breath, he hoisted up his bag and set his sights on the cars speeding down the highway.

"Mind the road," I said, turning the van onto the lane leading to the gallery. Going on my way, replaying this peculiar encounter with an interesting wanderer of the highways, wondering if every now and then, the jolly red-cheeked traveler will remember today and think of me.

-*nine*-

Crossing the Virginia line, I noticed the wind slowed, reducing the frigid air to a more tolerable temperature as I drove leisurely along Main Street, Onancock. Christmas holiday decorations adorning storefronts warmly welcomed visitors. I rolled the van to a stop next to the gallery window and brought my art boxes inside the building in a hurry. Without wasting any more time, I finished up the necessary pleasantries, said my farewell, then steered towards my favorite Hospice thrift store located within a half mile of the gallery. I do have my priorities after all.

The Hospice outfit was my favorite up-market thrift shop operated by a team of dedicated volunteers. All proceeds benefit the organization's mission of providing for the needy. I find the second-hand store to be a treasure trove of nifty things I don't need. Squandering money in my favorite hunting grounds was my version of philanthropy. I like to think I did something good for humanity.

Poking through the variety of used trinkets is enormously cathartic, especially perusing the dog-eared book aisle, where for some unknown reason I was drawn to the children's book section. Off to the corner, *The Night Before Christmas* set on a large easel. I thumbed through the beautifully illustrated pages, admiring the artwork and stopped midway, stunned by an image. Clutching the book tighter, my hands began to tremble and my mouth fell wide open. Impossible as it may seem, there was no mistaking on page twenty-two in full techno color staring back at me. was my curious little hitchhiker. His exact face, round and cherry red, and his eyes a hypnotizing swirling crystal. For a moment, I thought he had winked at me. But that would be impossible. This was a silly children's book after all.

My cell phone rang from inside my jacket pocket causing my heart to skip a beat. It was Hank.

"Hi hon."

"Where are you?" he asked.

"I dropped off artwork at the gallery, then stopped at a thrift store. I'm heading home soon."

"You sound peculiar. Are you alright?"

"I don't know how to say this, but I think I just met Santa Claus."

"Un-huh, that's nice. Did you remember to stop at the store?" he asked.

I didn't remember. In fact, I blocked it from my mind altogether, but I wasn't going to tell him that.

"You didn't stop, did you?" he asked again in a hard tone.

"I was going there on the way home," I said, just a small fib that I would be punished for by serving my sentence running errands at Walmart. I'm beginning to believe that on some subconscious level I might be developing a deep-seated Walmart phobia.

"Please, don't forget. You can handle this one chore, can't you? It's not like you have that many responsibilities," Hank said. My husband's timbre suggested his exasperation with me.

"I won't forget," I sighed, steering the van towards Walmart. Lord knows I have had my fair share of unfortunate incidents at that store, and was not looking forward to adding another one to the list. I'm still angry with the manager who hastily blamed me as the one smoking marijuana in the soda aisle, when all I wanted was a six-pack of ginger ale. He called the police, who in turn conducted an interrogation until the store's surveillance tapes vindicated me. I was a hapless victim of circumstances, that's all. Why would I reduce myself to petty crimes when there's security cameras posted at every nook and cranny as an effective theft deterrent?

It's surprising, the large number of murder cases that are solved by Walmart's surveillance camera filming idiots purchasing their weapon just before committing monstrous acts. You have to hand it to the dopes for being thrifty-minded shoppers.

I don't think I can muster the strength to endure a Walmart shopping adventure today, tomorrow, or through the next millennium. With the way my luck tends to roll, the foot fetish man will be there, weirdly cruising the aisles for women and complimenting their feet. He had freaked me out on more than one occasion during the flip-flop season.

-ten-

Maneuvering the vehicle round the outskirts of Walmart's car lot, I parked in one of the few available parking spaces.

Great, the place is packed. Let the holiday pushing and shoving begin.

Girding my big girl panties, I sucked in a big breath, then walked inside the packed store, instantly knocked back a peg by the gaudy commercial decorations. The bright seizure-causing neon lighting made the garish holiday manifestation border on the surreal. Synthesized music tracks cackled overhead. Shopping aisles filled with cranky fitful children pitched tantrums, tormenting parents with every passing toy display. Overpowered by holiday stimulation, my heart palpitated in my chest as I mindlessly stuffed unnecessary items in the cart and proceeded to the crowded checkout lanes. The blue domed light at the number six checkout lane flashed *Open*, illuminating my way to freedom. The blue light also caught the attention of two other people. I raced my cart to the lane, beating them by a few seconds; an eighty-six-year-old man and a woman operating the store's electric scooter. Not a proud moment for me.

The cashier was in total agreement, judging by her scornful stare as she rang me up. I smiled politely at her, and then at the two losers in line behind me, and wheeled my victorious cart towards the exit door.

Passing by the restrooms, I stopped in my tracks dumbfounded by an image on the billboard mounted on the wall. Printed in bold attention-grabbing lettering, *Have You Seen This Child?* spanned the width of the billboard. Below were numerous portraits of smiley-faced children perfectly spaced apart. Due to nation-wide efforts, the billboard success rates are quite favorable in recovering missing children. Over eight-thousand children have been returned safely.

Studying the individual profiles, I took note of the abduction date and town where they were last seen. Each abduction occurred within a hundred miles of this very store, an immensely disturbing common denominator. Photographs of innocent faces blended into a single tragic profile, except for one. A girl with a red velvet ribbon holding hair in a ponytail, taken in a formal setting like a school portrait maybe. Her face was so familiar to me and yet I didn't remember where. Then it whacked me square between the eyes and I was never more certain of anything in my life. Though a much younger version, it was definitely her, the girl I picked up from Gas & Go Mart. My heart dropped inside my chest as her image receding in the van's rearview mirror looped in my consciousness. I should have tried harder to help. I should have kept her safe. My knees trembled, about to give way. My skin grew clammy, and I thought I might faint, or throw up, or both simultaneously, and I slouched over the cart.

My nauseated behavior alerted the store manager. He approached with caution, "Is there a problem here Miss?"

"No," I mumbled. He probably assumed I was high or under the influence. The last thing I need right now is Walmart calling my husband again, so I left the store in a hurried panic and the image of the girl's photograph blowing my brain apart. I would have been certain she's the same girl, except for knowing how a child's features shift rapidly until puberty before showing a glimpse of the adult to come. Still, the possibility of the girl being a run-away juvenile was very real. Regardless, I was not responsible for her welfare.

I had regained my composure by the time I reached the van, and felt able to pilot the vehicle with steady hands away from the Walmart shopping center to the house before Hank returned and started his coffee. I decided to bypass the caffeine rush and sat down at the table, anxiously awaiting him. My nerves were overloaded, and I didn't need the coffee. I'd much rather have a glass of my usual sedation, but it was a little early for that. It would be to my advantage speaking to my husband in a sober state of mind.

Hank walked through the door sensing tension in the house. He skipped the ritual fuss over the dogs and marched straight to the kitchen. With one look he instantly knew something was wrong by my mannerism.

"What is it now, Molly?" he asked, sitting down at the table with a quizzical concern plastered over his face, one that had become a very familiar expression to me.

Expanding my lungs with a large breath, I proceeded to spill everything about the Amber Alerts and the haunting photo, ending with picking up Santa Claus from the highway all in one breathless sentence. Once I started, I could barely get the words out fast enough.

"Don't worry about that girl, Molly. If you want, I will put in a call to Walt, not sure what good it will do. She's probably long gone by now."

"How can you be so sure about that?" I asked, sensing otherwise.

Hank stood, pulled out the wine opener from the drawer, then screwed the device into the bottle cork until I heard the welcome pop.

"Perhaps people like her really don't want to be found, for good, or bad reasons. Same goes for that Santa hitchhiker of yours. It sounds to me like he's thoroughly prepared and proficient at traveling in bad weather," he said, placing a wine glass on the counter and filling it three quarters full.

I studied my husband as he fished the bourbon bottle from the cabinet, filled a rock glass with ice, and then poured the golden liquid breaking over the frozen cubes. He turned and smiled. Hank has a way of dismissing my fears and slaying the Boogeyman in one fell swoop, and the glass of chardonnay he handed to me placed him in superhero status.

"I understand what you say, but I know something terrible happened to the Gas & Go Mart girl. You weren't there, Hank. You didn't see how she was running scared," I said, and swallowed the wine, anticipating the warm rush of calm.

"It's all right, Molly. I'll call Walt and have a talk with him first thing in the morning."

"You would have a better chance of getting him to listen than I ever will," I sighed.

"Isn't your buddy, Jules, on her way to the island?" Tuned to my mounting stress level, Hank successfully changed the subject.

"Julia despises when people call her Jules. I made that mistake once. How do you get away with it?"

"Because of my wit and charming personality."

"She adores you."

"I know," Hank grinned. "Why don't you try focusing on her visit. Spending time with Jules will cheer you up."

"The only purpose Jules has for braving this sort of inclement weather would be to go to that stupid Christmas party," I remarked with annoyance. "Did I ever tell you I hate parties?"

Julia was not only my good friend, but also very gifted at making everyone else feel better about everything. Our friendship had melded into a pile of alcoholic wine-driven impropriety with a sprinkling of shenanigans that kept us up all hours of the summer nights in hysterics. Regrettably, our friendship has been part-time since. Like many of the island life forms, Julia winters elsewhere, in Baltimore, returning with the first warming rays of sunshine in the spring. Her weekend home was the first house you saw when entering Smithtown. She had taught me the value of friendship, and how to shop for tasty, yet budget-friendly, wines. And on several occasions, I think I may have caught sight of a halo forming above her head.

"Yes, it's always fun with her," I said, not sure Hank was truly aware of what goes on at Julia's house.

Hovering over me, Hank kissed the top of my head, "I'm turning in," he said softly, then went upstairs for the evening. His winter mornings begin at the same ungodly hour as they do in the summer.

"What about dinner?"

"Thanks, I ate on the road. Try not to fall asleep on the couch again, Mol."

"I won't." Boy, oh boy, does my husband know me or what? With Hank out of sight, I slammed the surplus wine down my throat, waiting a few seconds for the buzz to kick in, then poured the second glass of sure-fire liquid tranquility. There are moments when life becomes too much for anyone to handle, especially one like mine. This should help wash away this crazy day.

In the front room, I wedged myself into the couch and felt around between the cushions until I found the remote, then switched on the television to find a football match in progress. The brightly colored team uniforms danced across the screen. Football, or sports in general, was not my area of expertise, nor do I wish it to be.

The wine stirred blurry memories of my father watching football in his den, the *Man-Cave* of that era. My mother claimed her own space in the room by growing her precious, but temperamental, African violets on the windowsill. In retaliation to my father's football obsession, she decided to follow figure skating on television and eventually yelled at the athletes on the screen with the same passion as my father.

I sank deeper inside the couch cushions, letting the wine work its magic, sipping lazily with heavy eyelids, until falling safely asleep.

* * *

"Mom, I thought you were dead," I gasped.

My mother smiled, "Yes, I'm still dead, dear."

She seemed younger than I remembered, roughly thirty years old. She was dressed in her favorite pink polyester suit sewn together on her Sears and Roebuck sewing machine she had purchased in downtown Trenton, New Jersey.

"Mom," I cried, folding my arms around her, "I miss you so much."

"Why? Look how well I'm doing, no more pain. There's no need for tears, young lady."

"Will you stay and never leave me?"

"Oh, Molly, you know I can't do that."

"I don't want you to go. I don't want to be here all alone." It felt as if every emotional experience I ever had in my life had melded into one giant ball of confusion.

"Sweetheart, you're never alone. Every moment you think of me I'll be right there filling that space in your heart." Smiling, my mother placed her soft, warm hand over mine, then began to whirl into a swirling eddy of light, and I became ten years old again, uncomplicated and pure, and completely content.

* * *

"Molly, wake up," Hank spoke gently, nudging my shoulder.

"Huh? I must have fallen out."

"You were hollering in your sleep, calling out for your mother." Hank moved the empty wine glass from the couch and set it upright on the end table, then sighed disapprovingly. "How many of these did you have?" he asked.

"Not many," I lied, wiping at the still damp wine stain spreading across my shirt. Lately, spilling my wine occurs more often than I care to mention.

"Come to bed hon, it's getting late."

"Yes, it is," I agreed, aware it was already too late for me.

-eleven-

Starting the morning off with a stiff scrubbing to the face usually thwarts any lingering hangover residue which has the sole purpose of ruining my day. I woke up dead tired, barely sleeping after dreaming about my mother.

I can't take much more of this.

My usual sleeping tricks, like counting the asbestos ceiling tiles, or imagining sandy white beaches with fluffy marshmallow waves breaking the shorelines, failed to summon a restful night. I even pulled out all the big guns, reciting multiple rounds of the *Lord's Prayer*. Still, nothing brought on that wonderful unconscious slumbering state.

Sometimes, I resort to self-medicating with wine and shots of cough syrup, even though I don't like the residual goofy haze feeling all the next day. Those are the worst hangovers. The hours drag on at a snail's pace.

I looked up at the wall clock, it was four-thirty already. What a total waste of a good day. At this rate the Gas & Go Mart girl's disappearance into the shadowy darkness will plague my every waking moment. I will suffer sleep deprivation until I know she's safe and far from harm. Hank may think I am overreacting, and maybe his attempt to disquiet my fears was done in earnest, but in the light of day, dread is assembling something reprehensible in strength. I can sense it in my bones.

From now on, I'll be running in full crazy-mode until I find out what *it* is. I'm positive the child pictured in the photograph at Walmart was the same girl I met at the Gas & Go Mart. The resemblance couldn't be denied.

I poured a cup of stale morning coffee into my Batman mug, saving the Wonder Woman mug for special occasions, and sat at the kitchen table rubbing my throbbing temples. Halfway through the black brew, I felt my body resurrecting, and my thoughts became clearer. There was only one person who could set me on the right course, and that would be my real-life superhero, Ray Burton, investigative columnist for the County Times newspaper. Like the singer-actress Cher, Burton rarely uses her full name, same goes for her story by-lines. Okay, perhaps Burton isn't a superhero, but her investigational skills are top notch in bringing down the bad guys, from corporate gluttony to child molesters. And to top it off, she looks banging in a pantsuit. On any other occasion, being in the presence of a woman like Burton, my inner bitch would have reared its ugly head and released jealous commentary in rapid fire succession. But not in this case. I want to be her when I grow up.

Scrolling through my contacts, I found her office information and tapped the number, waiting for someone to pick up. "Is Burton available?"

"Who?"

"Burton."

"Who did you say?"

"Burton, she's an employee there, a columnist, has the corner office."

"Oh, Ray, she's not here right now. She'll be back in on Thursday."

"Does she have a message box?"

"A what?"

"Somewhere I can leave her a message."

"Oh no, we don't have anything like that."

"How about voicemail, I'm sure you have that."

"No, but she'll be back here on Thursday."

"Can I leave her a note with my number so she can return my call?"

"Like I said, she returns Thursday."

If it were at all possible, I would reach through my phone and punch this person in the boob, and so would Burton if she knew the woman had referred to her as *Ray*.

"Can you tell her Molly Hanson called, it's important. She has my number," I growled and disconnected.

Less than two minutes later my cell buzzed. It was Burton.

"Hey Molly, long time no hear. My secretary paged me, said you called. What's up?"

"I was told you were out of office until Thursday."

"Sorry about that. What can I say, that's what you get when you hire temps. I'm swamped, drowning this very moment. I'm working a case involving numerous complaints about a man who gets his rocks off copping a feel in the spaghetti aisle at Walmart."

The sheer mention of that store made my ass cheeks clench.

"Sounds like that Foot Fetish Man had pushed his game up a step," I responded in a cool tone. The easy solution to stop the overactive touchy-feely foot person's activities, would be to just ban the guy from the store. I understand everyone has a right to their quirky preferences, but I think people need to keep their weirdness to themselves.

"So, tell me Molly, what's this call about? Do you have a hot tip for me?" Burton asked with her antenna hoisted at full mast.

"Nope, nothing like that. I thought you could rectify my situation that's now become an epidemic mind infection. I'm losing sleep over this."

"I'm all ears, let it rip."

"Are you familiar with a house that's directly across from the sheriff's department?"

"A weird place and hard to miss."

"That would be the one. What can you tell me about the guy who lives there?" I felt confident Burton would have the answer. Burton had the skinny on most people in this town, and was known to keep tabs on the extra squirrelly ones, especially the newly released parolees.

"Do you mean red-headed Robby?" Burton asked, in a voice pitching upward a few decibels.

"Wait, are you talking about the red-headed Robby with the club foot that owns a bunch of chicken houses?"

"No, no, I mean the other Red-headed Robby, the one that's a prime suspect in multiple petty theft cases. He picks up the odd repair job here and there, cases the joint then returns and robs the place when no one is home. It's pretty much common knowledge that Robby was the one committing the robberies, but they can't catch him in the act. The guy is slipperier than a new bar of soap in the shower. You didn't mention why you needed the info on red-headed Robby."

"No, it's not Robby. This guy is decked out in camouflage clothing, and there's not one red hair on his head. The thing is, I gave a lift to a girl who had run off after they had a big public blowout. I think she's a run-away and may be connected to those local Amber Alerts."

"Camo, you say? That doesn't narrow down the field very much, this is Somerset County after all. Everybody wears camo. Did the girl say why she was running, or anything about him?"

"She told me zippo. All I know about her is she was extremely upset with the guy. I tried making conversation, but that didn't work out too well. She insisted I stop and let her out of the car." During a pause in the conversation, I sensed Burton's eyebrow had cocked.

"You made her mad, didn't you, Molly? You can't go around making people mad and expect them to divulge information. Let me give you some advice. When mining evidence from a perp, always use discretion," she said. She must have switched focus to the computer screen, as I heard her long polished fingernails tapping the keyboard at lightning speed. I found the clicking mesmerizing. My one-finger typing looks like a chicken pecking at food in the yard.

"Yes, I understand your point now," I mumbled, my face flushing.

"I'll see what I can dig up on the guy and let you know."

"Thanks Burton, you are an absolute wiz. I knew you would help me with this. I was beginning to lose sleep over it." All the signs were now starting to add up, but to what I wasn't one-hundred percent sure. Up until now, the Gas & Go Mart girl, the non-red-headed Camo-Man, and the group of missing girls had caused a great deal of collateral damage in my mind. Dropping this in Burton's lap made it her problem, letting me purge all this clutter from my brain like a worthy mental vomit.

"I bet your buddy Walt knows more than he lets on. You should put the squeeze on him. I would do it for you, but he runs into his office and locks the door when he sees me pull into the department lot," Burton admitted.

"I know, he does the same thing to me."

"Is there anything else I can do for you Molly?"

"No, I'm good. Thanks again," I said

"Keep your head low, kiddo."

"Thanks, you do the same," I replied. My day was going nowhere fast. At least Megan refrained from phoning today. And on the upside, Julia would have landed in town two hours ago, and that meant a heavy forecast of wine was in my immediate future. In my time-zone, it's always half past wine o'clock.

I think I'll drive down to her house. Even though her place was conveniently located within walking distance, moving through the dimness of night with a heavy wine buzz was never a good idea. I should probably check and see if she's here first and give her a call.

Julia answered on the first ring,

"You here yet?"

"Yes, though I thought I'd never make it fighting the amount of holiday congestion on the roads. The city is wall-to-wall people until Christmas."

"Just another wonderful aspect of the holiday I can't stand. And it's not just Christmas, that goes for Hanukkah, Quanza or any other Hallmark-induced holiday. I'm tired of it, especially having fake cheery Christmas greetings shoved down my throat wherever I go, when the rest of the year people act like complete assholes."

"You're in a great mood."

"I'm sorry. Holidays are harder to deal with now that my parents are gone."

"I have wine."

"I'll be there in a minute."

I left another note on the table for Hank stating my whereabouts, though there was no need. Hank would see my van parked in Julia's driveway on his way home and wouldn't be expecting me. Time to cure this hangover with a little hair of the dog.

- twelve –

If at first Julia's Cape Cod style summer home had ever given the impression that its size was limiting, the abundance of charm would quickly rectify any perceived deficiency. The cottage was more than suitable for her weekend plans, and tastefully decorated as well.

In the warmer growing season, a stunning bed of red geraniums and bushy pink crepe myrtles welcome guests at her little white house with dark gray shutters. The front porch with its painted turquoise ceiling runs the width of the house where we sit on a marigold yellow two-seater bench watching the sun set. The building's an older structure, but not nearly as ancient as ours, and heated by a dependable baseboard heating system. Something I enjoy very much during our visits. It's the only time I am warmed to my core.

"Wasn't it Benjamin Franklin who invented wine?" I asked, sitting on her overstuffed couch waiting for a glass of wine to magically appear any second in my hand. I couldn't think of a more perfect way to end the day.

"Don't you remember anything you learned in grade school, or had you already started drinking wine back then? Ben Franklin tied the key to a kite?"

"Yes, I remember. He tied it so he wouldn't lose the key to the wine cellar," I answered, and Julia smacked her forehead.

"I find it incredibly fascinating how your mind operates. It's like a Petri dish. You never know what kind of fungus culture will spring from it." She left the living room for the kitchen to unpack two bottles of wine and placed them in the fridge.

"Do you need anything before we go?" Julia hollered out, surveying her empty cabinet shelves.

"Go where?"

"I was in such a hurry to come here, I forgot the food. We can take a ride while the wine chills to perfection."

"Glad you remembered the wine. I doubt there's anything worthy to eat at my house. Too bad, I just got comfy." I sank deeper into her couch.

"The cabinets are empty, winterized just like the house. There's not even a small crumb left to feed a mouse. This won't do at all."

And this was yet another reason why I value our friendship. Julia understands the most important essentials in life are junk-food and cheap wine.

"I'll drive," I said, springing upward and throwing my coat over my shoulders in one fell move.

Julia fished her car keys from her understated but fashionable purse. "No, I'll drive this round."

"Why can't I drive?" I asked, a little put off.

"It's best we take my car," she paused. "Look, there isn't another way to say this except in truth.

"Lay it on me."

"I don't like your car. It's covered in dog hair, greasy trash, and it reeks to the high heavens. I think you should give consideration to purchasing a newer car." Julia waved her hand at the door motioning for us to leave.

"No way, I'm keeping this baby until the wheels fall off," I said, defending my van's honor, even though the wheels falling off was a very real possibility.

"And that's another reason why I don't like your car. I may be riding in the darn thing when it comes apart!"

"Sure, maybe the van is ugly. The side panels are rusted through, and yellow foam falls from the ceiling like snow. Who cares if it makes a few scary noises. The engine runs smoothly and besides, it suits me."

"Who are you kidding? It sounds like Godzilla attacking Tokyo, and the French-fries wedged in the seats are a decade old," Julia laughed, still with a firm grip on her keys, not budging an inch on this one.

"Okay, you win, you can drive. Where are we going? The Gas & Go Mart I presume?"

"But of course," Julia affirmed. "It's the Mecca of junk-food, all housed under one roof."

"Sounds like the perfect plan, though I'd like to take a small detour on the way back, if that's alright with you."

"Molly, what harebrained scheme are you fixing to tangle up with now?" she asked with some caution as if knowing she wouldn't like the answer.

"Come on, I'll tell you in the car, there might be a little cavorting involved on your part."

"Why does your life always sound like a television soap to me?"

"I never thought of it that way. I see my life as more akin to action television, a savior of the universe type of show."

"Really? I was thinking more like the Three Stooges," she mumbled as she climbed into her car, but I still heard what she said.

Admittingly, riding along in Julia's brand-spanking-new, fuel-efficient, freshly scented, fully equipped ride with state-of-the-art options made for a pleasant ride. She certainly made a valid point, the van was an eyesore, but it didn't smell as bad as it once did with the rotted deer skull on the van's antenna.

It was shortly after the muzzleloader hunting season had ended, when I found the skull partially covered by oak leaves while walking in the woods. It was in the last stages of the decomposing process and I didn't want that odor in the car, so I decided to hang it on the passenger side antenna until I reached home. Problem being, I completely forgot about the deer head, and ran the van all over creation with the oozing skull dangling just beyond my line of vision. Julia has yet to recover from the wretched smell. I can't blame her for refusing to ride in the van.

Inside Julia's car, we snaked our way, winding around the marsh, crossed the three bridges, and onto the mainland in mundane chatter. Julia finally broke.

"Alright, spill it," she demanded.

"I'm not sure what you mean."

"Don't play coy with me. You're busting at the seams."

"Okay, but I don't know where I should start."

"Go with whatever comes to mind first."

"Alright then, I have a strong sense that the recent Amber Alerts are somehow connected to that strange house across the street from the Sheriff's Department. There's something illegal going on," I said, waiting a few seconds for her to bite. I didn't need to see my friend's face to know she was hooked. Her curiosity runs almost as deep as mine.

"Come on now. You don't know that to be true."

"Three women mysteriously vanished, and all were last seen in Somerville. The police believe the abductions are connected, and I'm sure that weird place is somehow involved." I let that enticing ditty set my trap.

"I'm beginning to think you watch too much television while under the influence. If you're going to make allegations like this, then you better have concrete proof. You could cause a lot of harm if you don't."

"I've personally seen women come and go from that house at unusual hours. They look young, maybe high school age. And before you go on about my imagination working double duty, Hank has seen them as well."

"Hank agrees with you?"

"Yes, to some extent."

"Well, that's a first."

"You can't deny the activities at that house appear shady. If only we could see past the drawn curtains."

Julia had to believe me now. In her eyes, Hank walks on water. Same goes for all the women who know my husband.

"No crime in having visitors, is there?" she asked.

"I suppose there isn't, but you don't know the whole story. Walt said the authorities suspect the missing women are linked in some way, and I believe the connection includes the missing girl from Fairview and that house."

"Oh, I heard about that, very sad news, and so close to home. Mrs. Stone is such a nice lady. She must be ruined with worry over that granddaughter of hers."

"I didn't realize you knew her that well."

"We both volunteered for the firehouse oyster dinner fundraiser, she's very friendly. I heard the police originally thought that her granddaughter had just run away. I could see that being the case, teenage hormones steer the young in every misdirection."

"You seem to know more than I do," I noted, surprised.

"It's amazing how local news travels the distance to Baltimore in record time. Poor Mrs. Stone, I wish there was something I could do." Julia's face altered into a blank expression. Tragedies occurring this close to Smithtown are harder to digest than when hearing it on the news.

This is real, and spreading fear like wildfire. It's impossible to ignore or hide it in the shadowed areas of our mind.

"There's more," I said.

"Am I going to be able to handle it?" Julia questioned.

"I haven't told you about the girl that was begging for money at the Gas & Go Mart. She had a huge argument with that camo dude who lives in the house I mentioned. The two of them were shouting in the parking lot until the girl had enough and took off down the road. I found her walking on four-thirteen and offered her a ride."

"Wait a minute, I think I know the guy you're talking about. I've seen that man before. He wears a camo-hoodie, twenty-four-seven?"

"Yes, that's him. The guy could easily stand in the middle of a crowd in the bright mid-afternoon and be perfectly camouflaged like a weed in the fray."

"Hold on, let's back up a bit. What are you doing picking up strangers?"

"It was too dark and dangerous for her to be walking that road at night. You know what it's like. Chances are she would have been hit by a car."

"I can hardly see a thing on that road, even when I'm driving with my high beams turned on."

"I'm afraid I wasn't much help to the girl. She acted fairly belligerent towards me. She demanded to be let out of the van. All I could do was watch as she vanished into the night. I still feel dreadful about that."

"But in reality, what could you do? The girl has a mind of her own, and you had no say in the matter."

"Thanks. I know you have good intentions, but I don't feel any better about her well-being."

"If you want my advice, Molly, you can't do anything about whatever is going on in that house, or with that troubled girl. I believe, in your case, the best course of action would be to let the authorities do their job."

It didn't take long for Julia to form an opinion about my running head-first into yet another asinine adventure.

"And for future reference," she began, "Don't even think about asking me to go peeking in his windows, though you probably have already. Whatever it is you decide, I prefer that it doesn't involve me."

"I'll heed your advice and forget all about the girl," I replied to my friend with assurance, but in all actuality, I knew forgetting about the girl would never happen in a million years.

-thirteen-

We executed our trek to the Gas & Go Mart convenience with a prickly air between us. Judging by the glare Julia shot me sideways, I'd say she had more than her fill listening to my conspiracy theories. She had every right to react this way considering how many times I put her in compromising situations. Trespassing, destruction of property, and public disturbance to name a few.

"I hope what I'm about to say doesn't come off sounding like a lecture, but you have a tendency to get yourself into sticky wickets that leave me drowning in your quicksand," she stated.

"You're overreacting."

"I am not."

"It's not like my motives are devious in nature. Besides, you like the excitement, don't you? Tell the truth."

"Sometimes yes, I do like the thrill. I will admit that."

"And your curiosity is piqued right now, isn't it?

"Alright, you got me there. I just don't want either of us getting into trouble. Molly, you need to look twice before you leap. And that, my friend, is the crux of all your problems. You never look before diving headfirst into the shallow end," said Julia. Using the turn signal, she pulled into the Gas & Go Mart car lot, then turned her new car's engine off. "Why don't we forget about this foolishness for now and go choose snacks that would best match chilled white wine. I need to pick up a few other items for the house. I trust you can handle the food?"

"I guess so," I answered stiffly, as if I was a scolded child, and followed her inside the store.

As always, Yusuf was working the long shift. I swear that man has a canvas cot he sleeps on in the storage room.

"You're back so soon Molly. Need more junk-food? I also sell fruit. You should try it sometime," he smiled.

"Thanks, but it's for my friend." I said, covering for my bad habit, then proceeded to poke through the aisles, making various unhealthy choices.

Julia, on the other side of the store, made her final selections then went to the register where I waited.

"You good?" she asked.

"No, I forgot the ice cream, I'll just be a sec," I said, dumping the contents in my arms onto the counter, then jogged over to the frozen delights section.

"Ice cream doesn't pair well with wine. Come on, Molly, we have plenty to eat right here," Julia begged.

Ignoring her plea, I equipped myself with two Klondike Bars and a quart of Rocky Road from the freezer. Armed and ready, I turned for the counter and slammed full-steam into the Camo-Man's chest.

I looked up, his expression more solid, and colder than the ice cream I dropped on the floor. My mouth opened slightly, producing a pathetic squeaky gasp. Side stepping past, I took off with my heart pounding faster than my feet were hitting the linoleum floor.

"Come on," I grabbed Julia's elbow, "We have to leave, right now."

"Wait, what about the ice cream?"

"They're all out of ice cream," I said, rushing her out the door.

"What's going on? What's happening?"

"Come on, hurry up."

"What's the big rush?"

"He's not home."

"Who's not home?"

"Camo-Man. I just ran into him in the freezer section."

"Well, isn't that a brilliant deduction on your part, bravo!"

"No need to be snide."

"Oh, I think there is."

"I want to make a quick stop at his house."

"Whatever for? Never mind, I don't care to know. I'm not doing it anyway."

"It'll be three minutes, tops."

"Oh boy, here we go again," Julia sighed, totally aware resisting would be useless, and directed her car towards the creepy house across from the Sheriff's Department building.

"Pull over on the shoulder, right before his house, then cut the car lights." I sat upright, gripping the dashboard. Julia hummed one of the James Bond theme songs until falling into a belly laugh.

"Be quiet now, this isn't funny," I said, giggling along with her.

As I instructed, Julia slowed her car and turned off the lights. Stones crunched and popped under the tires.

"Stop right here, that's close enough."

"I am afraid to ask, but do you have a plan?"

"I thought I would just have a look around."

"For what?"

"I dunno."

"Are you coming with me, or what?"

"Hell no."

"Keep a lookout then."

"For what?"

"I dunno."

"Don't you find this conversation redundant?" Julia shook her head.

"It held me in total suspense," I answered, exiting the car, and then quietly shut the door. I stood a moment, scoping the perimeter of the house before approaching, as my intestines pitched in waves. I noticed that the house was dimly lit, and I would need to move much closer to see anything. Luckily, the windows were set low, giving me a clear view to most of the first level rooms.

Skulking along the side of the house, I came to the first window and pressed my face against the glass to see what must have been the living room. It was sparsely furnished with a shabby couch, a couple of end tables, and an armchair that had seen better days. On the wall, hung a classic paint-on-velvet picture of dogs playing poker over a small flat screen television that sat on a plastic milk crate. The room struck me as unremarkable.

"Hurry up! I'm getting cold," Julia hollered out from the car window.

"Shush!" I held up my hand, signaling her to wait, then dipped behind the house into total obscurity. Maneuvering the ill-lit yard was scary and difficult. With my luck, I would trip over and face-plant into something hard. I let my toes lead the way, inching through the dead grass and around the hunks of rusting metal, until reaching the last window, and pressed my nose against the smudgy glass.

Dangling from the ceiling center, a green light bulb cast a strange eerie glow over the pool table and on every other flat space in the room. Metal folding chairs lined the wall, and empty beer bottles were splayed about the perimeter. Nope, nothing out-of-the-ordinary to see here. I figured by now that Julia would be worrying her knickers into knots. I should head back before she starts yelling again. I gave the room one more scan and my eyes fell short on the farthest wall. In reduced lighting, it took several moments for my mind to register that it wasn't a wall, but a door dead-bolted and locked from the inside, and painted to blend with the wall color. I moved around searching for where the door would be located, then ran my hands over mismatched asphalt siding.

This didn't make any sense. I thought there had to be a way to enter from the outside, and continued sneaking around the yard. The snapping sound of dead winter weeds crunching underfoot rang out into the night. My heart jumped with each crack. Tiptoeing onward, I came upon a kitchen window where a plug-in nightlight provided ample illumination for me to assess the room, and spotted a dog door flap installed on the back door.

I scurried around to the hatch, ruminating for a split second, whether or not this was the right thing to do, then stuck my head through the flap then wiggled, managing half my body inside. The sour stench of wet dog filling my nostrils was followed by a moppy-headed mutt that licked my face.

"Good doggie," I stuttered, as dog slime drizzled down my nose.

The dog arched his back and growled fiercely behind curled lips and bared teeth. Panic set in. I pushed with all my might backwards, getting stuck by my shoulders. The realization that I was trapped halfway through the dog hatch brought a rush of clarity to my situation. I was screwed.

The mongrel repeated his snarling with quivering lips that released a wad of slobber stretching down to the floor.

"Good doggie," I whispered slowly, getting ready for my face to be ripped off, and closed my eyes. Then I felt something abruptly grab hold of my ankles before yanking me free from the dog hatch.

"Seriously? What on earth do you think you're doing? Do you want to add breaking and entering to your resume? I swear there are times when I just don't understand you, Molly Hanson. Can we please go home now? It's getting colder by the minute. I have had more than enough of your shenanigans for one evening," Julia complained, stomping her feet all the way to her car.

"Technically, I didn't break in," I said, trampling behind, trying to keep up with her agitated swift pace.

"I'm not arguing semantics with you. Let's just go."

"Wait, stop and listen for a minute. Did you hear that?"

"I didn't hear anything. Your ears are ringing from squeezing your head through that hole."

"Wait, there it goes again. You mean to tell me you can't hear that? The sound is faint, but it's clear as a bell."

"Oh, it's just your fertilizer imagination."

"Don't you mean fertile imagination?" I asked, confused.

"No, I meant fertilizer because you're full of shit," Julia snapped.

"Did I ever tell you that it's your honesty I admire the most about you, brutal but honest?"

"Let's go home. I have a nice bottle of chardonnay calling my name, and that I can hear loud and clear for sure," Julia huffed.

"You're right, we should get out of here," I said, brushing the damp dirt from my clothes. "Phew, that was a close one."

"This isn't my idea of fun. You could have been torn to pieces by that nasty dog."

"I know, thanks."

"You are welcome, but please don't expect me to ever do it again."

"I won't, I promise. I'm probably blowing this all out of proportion. I bet there's a sensible explanation."

"An explanation for what? There isn't anything to explain."

Julia was right, I had nothing to go on. "I dunno," I sighed, falling into the passenger's seat.

Julia slammed her car door shut, and then turned the ignition key over with a shaky hand, letting the engine idle as she collected her nerves. No guessing about it, her perturbation with me was serious this time. On my next adventure, I might have to reconsider dragging her along.

Across the street at the Sheriff's Department, Walter had just begun his evening rounds when he caught sight of us parked in front of the creepy house. We were two dumb-ass deer caught in the cruiser's headlights.

"You have got to be kidding me," he grumbled out the open window. Sliding the cruiser in behind us, he hit the high beams, lighting up the interior of Julia's car. I turned around squinting at the headlights' beaming-bright rays.

Walter struggled with his sore knees emerging from the patrol car and gingerly walked towards Julia's car with his Maglite shining at the back of our heads. He gave a rap on the driver's side window. Julia refused to look up at him and kept her eyes straight ahead, hiding like a rabbit behind a blade of grass.

"Make no mistake, girlfriend," she growled. "If I get a ticket for this, I'm going to kill you the minute we get back and then bury your body where no one will find it."

"You'll have to wait your turn to do that," I answered, indignant.

"Evening ladies," Walter had one hand on his hip, and the other held the flashlight pointed at our reddened faces.

"Walt," I nodded.

"Would it be safe to assume you're having car trouble and that I should offer to call a tow truck? Or possibly you're lost and find yourself in need of directions. My other option would be to ask why you're sitting here in front of this house. But you see,"

Walter paused, then inhaled deeply, "Truthfully, I don't want to know, because if I did know then I'd have to arrest you, file a report, and then make that dreadful call to Hank about his wife's arrest. I would hate doing that. I like Hank, he's a good man. Now listen up, I don't ever want to see either of you two here ever again. Are we clear?"

"Crystal," I answered.

"Go home, please, just go without another word." Walter turned away, shaking his head.

Eager to obey Walter's no-word commandment, Julia slammed her new car into gear, then burned rubber making an illegal U-turn towards Smithtown, and hauled her new car far over the thirty-five mile-per-hour speed limit.

Disregarding the bold move, Walter led his cruiser in the opposite direction, probably shaking his head all the way down the highway.

"I can't believe he caught us," Julia said, now distraught.

"Caught us doing what? For all he knows, we were just innocently parked on the side of the road."

"I am so embarrassed."

"The only reason why you should feel embarrassed is because you were caught by Walt," I said, also embarrassed. Of all the cops in this world, why did it have to be him who showed up at that precise moment?

First thing tomorrow morning, Walt will blab to Hank about seeing us at the house, if he hadn't called him already. No worries, I still had a while to come up with a believable cover story.

-fourteen-

Still fuming, Julia refused to engage, or grunt a single syllable. She did, however, release several angry breaths. If I could have seen her face well enough, I'd bet it was red and blotchy. Julia was not the first person in the world to give me the silent treatment.

After three whole minutes traveling on a pitch-dark road without a word passing between us, I couldn't take it any longer and caved.

"When did the road become this long?" I asked, with hopes of renewing communication.

"It certainly feels that way tonight, painfully long in fact." Julia gave another sideways glare, confirming her annoyance. I needed to mend our bond.

"Piece of gum?" I asked, trawling around inside my coat pocket for the pack, then popped a piece in my mouth. Any debacle I find myself in, chewing gum always makes it better.

"No thank you," she snapped.

"You sure? It's Juicy Fruit, America's favorite gum."

"After what you put me through tonight, I'd rather drink every bottle of wine left in the fridge, including that left-over stale wine way in the back."

"Do you think we would still be good friends if we didn't have a common interest in alcohol?"

"Hard to say." Despite my excellent humor, Julia refrained from smiling.

"I'm sorry I made you detour to that house, and I'm sorry that Walt found us there. I'm sure he thinks we're up to something."

"Well, we *were* up to something."

"It was fun. And no one was hurt or arrested."

"I'd have to say, I do like our adventures," she added, as a small smile of forgiveness began to form over Julia's mouth, and I felt instant relief.

"I'll keep that in mind."

"And by the way, you haven't said a thing about what you saw in that house," reminded Julia. And just like that the awkwardness between us disintegrated.

"Except for the furniture dating to an ugly period, I thought the house was pretty normal until I walked around further."

"No kidding." Julia, trapped like a fly in the spider's web, asked, "What else did you see?"

"There was a side room that had a pool table in the center."

"Wow, that is suspicious!"

"No need to be flippant."

"Sorry, please continue."

"Just before leaving, I checked the room once again and saw a door that I missed before, and I also noticed it was dead-bolted shut. Obviously, someone didn't want anyone to enter or leave by that door. I walked around to where the door would have been located."

"What did you see?"

"That's just it, there wasn't anything to see. I looked but couldn't find the door anywhere."

"Now that's weird. Why would someone have a door that goes nowhere?" she asked.

"Precisely what I thought and decided to go inside the house to find out where the door led."

"In case you didn't know, breaking and entering is illegal. It's called a B&E in police lingo."

"Technically speaking, it wasn't a break-in since the hatch was already open. In reality, I never entered the house because I was wedged halfway in the dog door," I stated as if it were the truth, though I doubt that defense would hold much ground in court.

"I think after saving you from the dog door, you owe me one."

"I owe you two."

Without breaching any more laws, we rolled smoothly into Smithtown and into the house, safe and sound. Julia popped open the bottle of Chardonnay within seconds of entering through the front door. She fetched two glasses from the cabinet, filling hers to the brim, and downed the wine in three gulps all before removing her coat. The glass of wine did little to satisfy her nerves, and she poured another before offering a glass to me.

"Are you alright?" I asked with some concern. Her character had completely changed, and I almost didn't recognize my friend.

"This has been quite the night. Let's *not* do this again sometime." Still harboring these sentiments of ill will, Julia made a grand toasting gesture with her wine glass.

It's a given, that by the second glass of wine the truth will emerge in all its shameful glory. Changing the subject could aid our strained situation.

"I hope I never get another one of those Amber Alerts again. Two alerts close together is troubling," I said.

"I know what you mean. Living in Baltimore, I receive several a week. That's big city living for you." Julia sighed.

The room grew silent again. We both knew beyond the sanctity of Smithtown, the world out there was not all sunshine and rainbows, and often a scary place, more so than ever now for children.

"Did you know that the Amber Alert system was developed after a little girl who was abducted from her front yard? Four days later, they found her body in a ditch not far from her home."

"Good Lord, Molly, why do you know about this stuff?"

"I read it somewhere. It's an acronym for America's Missing Broadcast Response. Since the Amber Alert emergency response service is now standard on all cell phones, the recovery success rate has risen tremendously. The system targets a specific area where the child abduction was reported."

"Let's talk about something else before I end up like you and won't be able to sleep a wink tonight," said Julia.

"Last night, I dreamt about my mom again, do you want to hear it?"

"Yes, anything is better than discussing statistics about kidnapped children."

"My dream felt so real, and when I woke up, I thought I smelled her perfume. I could swear she was right there in the room with me. Sometimes, I think the dreams are because she's trying to make contact from the great beyond. Do you think that's possible, or that I'm just plain crazy?"

"The answer's both. I think you're nuts and I think of the human brain as an untapped resource. There's no telling what kind of power the mind possesses, or of its capabilities. Maybe dreams are an avenue for some kind of cosmic spiritual element to come through."

"Interesting theory," I said.

"There's another school of thought."

"What's that?" I asked.

"Some people believe that dreams are God's way of checking in," Julia added. "It's a comforting idea I suppose."

"And for some like me, I thank God there's wine. Like Benjamin Franklin said, wine was proof that God wants us to be happy," I raised my glass.

"He said that about beer," Julia corrected. "It was Thomas Jefferson who said that wine is the necessity of life."

"Either way, here's to iron livers, or the cure for cirrhosis of the liver. I can't imagine forgoing wine for any reason. I'd have to stick my head in the oven for sure." The sobering thought popped into my mind unwelcomed.

"But you couldn't commit suicide by oven."

"Why not?"

"Because it's full of wine bottles?"

"It's a mortal sin to let that wine go to waste."

"Ah yes, the eternal condemnation penalty," Julia smiled.

Between our conversation circling back and forth between subjects and the fast wine consumption, my eyes began to weigh heavy. I checked the time on the wall clock. It was hard to believe the alcohol-infused hilarity had continued into the late hour of midnight. I enjoy Julia's company because we can laugh for hours on end about nothing.

"How did it get so late?" I asked.

"Is it late?" Julia responded through a slight, but noticeable yawn, and that was my prompt to leave.

"It's way past my bedtime. I should leave while I can still walk. Thanks again for rescuing me tonight."

"Well, somebody had to do it. At least Walt didn't slap us both with a vagrancy fine."

"Better luck next time," I laughed heading out the door.

Though Julia's house was close by, I thought it wise to leave the van parked in her driveway and hoof my way home. No need in taking the chance of dumping the vehicle in the marsh because of a wine buzz, though I wouldn't be the first to put their car in the drink. On the island, it's considered a rite of passage.

I stepped out into the late-night coolness, taking in a frosted breath laced with woodsmoke. The air bit sharply at my lungs. Steadying my wobbly feet, I leaned my head back to gaze at the sky so clear and honest. Across the Sound, the stars reflected atop the sparkly waves. Watching them move in unison sent a stimulated feeling washing over my inebriated body.

Within a few minutes of bumbling down the road, I reached our house guided by my illuminated garden art sculptures along the brick walkway. I stood staring at the brilliant color bouncing over the broken sharp edges, pleased with myself for adding aesthetic value to our humble abode.

Inside the house, my footing was careful, though unnecessary because Hank sleeps like the dead. Dogs barking, cell phones ringing, or even his own explosive snoring fails to disturb his slumbering state. I wish I could relax like everyone else in the world. But that rarely happens. Stripping my clothes off, I let them lay in place on the floor, and then did a face-plant down on the bed. My head spun in orbit around the room. I'd pay the price in the morning by suffering through a banging headache the whole day, and would deserve every bit of it. Bam jumped up on the bed snuggling against me. He stretched out his legs and passed wind. That dog has no shame.

I rolled over with my eyes wide open to maintain equilibrium. It helped somewhat. I tried envisioning pretty green fields and butterflies, but nothing could hold back my thoughts from wading into the bleak darkness surrounding the Gas & Go Mart girl. I pressed my head into the pillow counting the passing minutes until every negative festering image dispersed from my mind, allowing room for sleep.

-fifteen-

The ringtone shot through my swollen brain like a bolt of lightning. "Oh good, you're alive," said Julia, calling on her cell phone. I wondered if you made it home last night in one-piece. I thought maybe you fell into the marsh." I rubbed my eyes, making another mental note to remember to cut back on the vino.

"I think I'm in one piece, except my head's a bit blurry this morning," I said, recalling I had left my van at her house.

"Sounds to me like you should take two aspirin and eat something."

"There's three-day old pizza in the fridge that should do the trick. I'll have a slice and a coke to wash it down."

"That sounds disgusting."

"It's one of my many hangover remedies," I mumbled, stifling a building yawn.

"You didn't get much sleep last night, did you?"

"No, it was rather fitful. I don't care anymore. Sleeping is overrated. It's only good as practice for when you're dead. I figured on honing that skill much later in life."

"You should try a nap. I find them refreshing."

"Napping is for sissies." I stated, and Julia chuckled.

"It might help if you stop drinking wine."

"What would be the point of living then?"

"Let's get back to the issue of your insomnia. What are you going to do about it?" Julia was spot on. I had entered into a severe sleep deficit several nights ago. "I would consider a nap if it didn't feel like short snatches of death."

"That's ridiculous."

"I'm a light sleeper. I wake up when Hank rolls over, or the dog farts. I might as well not bother with sleeping at all. How am I supposed to get any rest when the Gas & Go Mart girl, the Camo-Ma, and his creepy house are marching on my brain every night?"

"I wish I could help."

"Maybe you can, if you let me ask you a question." Rarely would I lay my soul out on public display. But Julia, who's smart and sensible, would never take advantage of my vulnerability. Sharing my load just might put an end to the marching band in my head.

"As long as it doesn't involve one of your schemes, then sure, ask away," Julia replied, her words coated with apprehension.

"No, it's nothing like that.

"What is it then?" she asked.

I waited a moment, weighing whether or not it would be a wise decision roping her into my mental madness. It's not how I roll. I thought better of it and changed course.

"Never mind, we'll talk again later. I'm going to take Bam for a walk this morning. You are welcome to come on with us."

"I'll have to pass. I'm painting my bathroom today." Julia had a penchant for purchasing gallons of paint that would sit unused, eventually forgotten and left to dry into a hardened blob in the can. It would be highly unusual for her to commit to a color.

She had experienced this same paint sampling process numerous times before. It's the reason why her walls tend to look like a patchwork quilt.

"Go enjoy your walk," Julia said, then disconnected.

"On my way back, I'll move my van out of your driveway."

After disconnecting, I dressed for the elements. Late morning chilly walks are ideal to clear the cobwebs. I'll forget every little thing that has been bothering me, if only for a short while. I called for Bam and fastened the leash around his neck. Bringing Sara Jane on lengthy walks had proved overly strenuous on her old body. In Labrador years, Sara Jane was as old as dirt. All she can manage are a few laps around the house on her arthritic legs. With her health declining so rapidly, it's a wonder she's still with us. During her last veterinary check-up, we were handed a grim prognosis that Sara Jane was living on borrowed time.

I bent low, running a light hand over her body, she stretched under my touch, then drifted contently asleep. For seventeen years, Sara Jane has been an integral part of our life. She's also the longest relationship I've had, including my marriage. When Hank told me he had pre-arranged cremation services for Sara Jane at the funeral home in Somerville to help ease the transition I became upset. But in hindsight, I'm grateful he handled everything in advance. Even though my resolve may be as steady as a rock, I wouldn't have that kind of strength.

In more benevolent weather, Hank and I will run the crab boat through the scenic route, cutting in-and-out of the winding marsh gut to spend the day on Oyster Island. The vibrating engine noise stirs the golden-eyed gristle shad to pop the water's surface several feet into the air. Oyster Island is Sara Jane's favorite place to swim and chase *minnas* along the sandy shores, while Bam scares sea birds crying into the air. Hank mulls around in black mud gathering immature oyster spat to raise in the cove, as I take it all in. This is my happy place filled with memories I return to often. It's the one place in Somerset County where I truly feel I belong. Hank and I decided when that dreadful hour comes for Sara Jane, it is Oyster Island where her ashes will be set free.

Leaving Sara Jane behind, I walked Bam down the road, passing by the cluster of tall pine trees where the wind whistles between the needled branches searching for a tune. Slow but steady, I regained stamina from the brisk exercise pumping fresh air into my lungs and brain cells, and was in total recovery before reaching the second bridge. I stood staring at the powerful tidal currents rushing past, amazed at how similar they seem to my world being pulled out of orbit. There was that distinct possibility my imagination could have distorted the truth. I've been known to spiral out of control and dive head first into trouble without considering any other possibilities. I should knock it off right now before I make a rash mistake. My problem was how to let go of the Gas & Go Mart girl and forget worrying about her welfare. That would never happen, and neither will I be cutting back on wine. Julia was insane for suggesting the idea in the first place.

I rested my elbows on the railing, watching ripple ringlets spread wider and felt my body unpin, relaxing to a peaceful easy sensation to my very core. What was the point of obsessing about the runaway girl, or the creepy house and its door to nowhere, or the Camo-Man and missing women? There's absolutely no reason for me to be this emotionally concerned, it's not my style.

I heard the vibrating ping sounding from my phone and slid it from my pocket and read the information regarding another Amber Alert. I felt sick and fought the urge to hurl the cell phone into the Sound. But then it came to me in a flash. This was it, the answer I needed smacked me between the eyes. And just like that my obsession had transformed into a mission. I looked around for Bam who was busy sniffing the guard rails deciding which one to pee on.

"Let's go boy," I said, jogging towards Julia's house as fast as I could in my out-of-shape status. Bam loped at my side, unfazed by my heavy breathing all the way down the road to Julia's driveway and piled into the van. I waited a moment for oxygen to replenish my lungs before turning over the engine, then gave Julia's house a honk goodbye with a long blast of the horn. She came to the window wearing a puzzled look planted across her face as I waved, backing the van from her driveway in a hurry. I had no doubt Julia had recognized the source of my excitement as a newly hatched harebrained idea, and I bet a little part of her felt a twinge of regret for not joining in.

-sixteen-

Recklessly speeding away from Smithtown, I kept the pedal to the floor mat, blurring the great span of marshes into one singular color, and flew around the S-turn with the confidence of a seasoned racecar driver. On the long stretch of road leading to the highway, I continued piloting the van onward, straining the engine at a good clip, and made it to the punch-and-run connection for route-thirteen north in no time. When passing both the sheriff's office and the creepy house, I avoided temptation by diverting my eyes. It was absolutely imperative for me to be at the Somerville fast-food restaurant as soon as possible if I wanted to catch Walter and squeeze him for information. Guaranteed at this hour that Walter's would be inside the fast-food joint busy stuffing his face and wouldn't see my ambush coming. Despite the fact that his duty preferences veer towards serving court summonses, he stays abreast on all the latest police business. If luck is with me, I'll have the answers I so desperately seek. All it takes with him is a food bribe.

Upon hitting the access road, I punched the gas pedal, gaining ground. Bam sat up front in the passenger's seat totally focused on the road as if he were the one driving. Unnerved by my snappy stunt car maneuvers, he dug his nails deep into the upholstery.

Up ahead, traffic slowed to a crawl, and I was staring at a sea of red brake lights. I strained my neck to see the obstacle impeding travel, and then smelled the issue. The very same garbage truck that previously held up traffic was on the job again. One by one, the line of vehicles passed by the cumbersome vehicle. Creeping along, I decided to stay put behind the truck, hidden in the mirror's blind spot. With each stop the garbage truck dispensed a rotted stench wafting inside the air vents, saturating the interior of my van. Nauseating diesel fumes mingled with the trash odor, and I thought I might hurl.

The truck paused at the creepy house, its brakes squealing and hissing under the massive vehicle. The driver set the diesel engine to idle, hopped out, walked to the rear of the truck, and began working the compactor controls running his routine, emptying the trash bins. The driver chuckled, amused by a plastic shopping bag that escaped the compactor and was now soaring high into the cobalt-blue sky. When he finished returning the trash bins to their curbside position, he climbed inside the truck and beeped the horn as he pulled away. I turned to see who he was signaling and caught sight of Camo-Man standing with arms folded on his porch. He gave a two-finger tick wave in response, as if he had been waiting for the driver. How could I have missed Camo-Man? I must be getting rusty.

My cell rang from my pocket, and I jumped in my seat, banging the side of my head on the driver's side window. The commotion set my heart thumping inside my chest. I fished out the cell phone and answered without checking caller ID. I was past due for a Megan call and figured it had to be her.

"Hello," I answered, pressing a hand over my heartbeat as it slowed to a normal sinus rhythm.

"I got a name for you." It was Burton, who sounded like she was wound tighter than a heavy metal rock band's drum head.

"I'm ready."

"Gordon Myers. Somehow, the guy was able to obtain employment at the Somerset County hospital. All I can say is the hospital must be desperate, or Myers lied on his resume and forgot to mention his six-month obligation at the Somerset County Correctional Facility for three consecutive driving offenses while under the influence of drugs and alcohol."

"I'm sitting in my van looking at Camo-Man as we speak. Do you know anything else about him, like where he came from, or why he's hanging out with girls almost half his age?"

"I'm working on it, still digging around in the dirt," she said, stressed. "Myers hangs around with low-lifers, they all have petty theft and drug distribution charges."

"Thanks, I appreciate it. His name is certainly as good a place as any to start."

"Go talk to Walt, I still think he's your best source. I'm sure he can fill in the blanks. In the meantime, I'll keep poking around."

"I'm on the way to see Walt, and he hasn't a clue I'm coming. It's a surprise attack."

"Sounds like the perfect plan. Until I can find out more about Myers, keep a safe distance. Gotta ring off, I have a load of work to tackle before the end of day. Take care," Burton disengaged the call before I had a chance to thank her. The woman puts a whole new spin on the meaning of high-strung, and if she doesn't take it down a notch she might launch into full-blown cardiac arrest. I used to think Burton would be a good match for Walter, and had briefly considered fixing the two up. They say opposites attract, but not polar opposites.

Ruminating on the new information Burton just handed me, I drove with mission on point, following the garbage truck through two more miles of fermented choking air. The trash vehicle turned off the road, and I went north towards the Somerville intersection where the high golden arches proudly tower over the highway. I turned again into the fast-food lot and as predicted, there was Walter's cruiser parked close to the entrance. There are many things in life you can always count on, like death and taxes, and the occasional flat tire, and that Walter never deviates from his schedule. In fact, the Universal Time Coordinated systems can be set by his daily routines.

Through the restaurant's large window glass, I could see Sheriff Wide-Man squatting in his favorite corner booth scarfing down his giant burger, vanilla milkshake, and a large bag of fries in solitude. I parked next to the squad car, then slinked my way to the restaurant door as Bam screamed bloody murder, a habit of his I can't seem to break. This particularly bad behavior was a real head turner, one that had once caught the attention of a state trooper who cited me for disturbing the peace. And of course, the incident happened at Walmart.

Inside the double doors, I walked over to Walter and plopped down on the bench facing him.

He looked up from his meal in shock and disappointment all in one emotion. I almost felt sorry for him.

"What do you want now?" mumbled Walter through a mouthful of food.

"I thought you could use some company."

"Whatever it is, you can just forget it right now," he said, taking a large bite of his sandwich, absolutely determined to enjoy his lunch.

"You're going to tell me everything you and the police know about the three Amber Alert texts I received on my phone. And when we're done with that, you're going to tell me all you know about the Camo-Man who lives in the creepy house across from your office."

"No way."

"Aw, come on Walt, the women's disappearances aren't just some random coincidences. You tell me first, and then I'll tell you what I know."

"Damn it Molly, you've been talking to Burton again, haven't you?"

"What's it to you if I did?"

"Stay away from that woman. Burton's a classic trouble maker that wreaks havoc with her damn newspaper articles."

"Gee Walt, and I was going to fix the two of you up."

"Don't even think about it."

"Alright then, let's resume our conversation about the disappearances."

"No way, I'm not getting into it with you, this here's police business. However, I am glad to see you."

"Since when have you ever been glad to see me?"

"I can't think of one single reason why I would be, but you happened to save me a trip hunting you down."

"Go ahead, Walt, lay it on me." I was ready and willing to lock horns with the jerk-faced sheriff.

"There's an important matter I'm officially required to discuss with you."

"Whatever it is, it's not my fault. I didn't do anything."

"This time it's not about you. The complaint was made against your dog. Your neighbor came barging into my office saying the dog had been relieving himself on her backdoor steps."

"Are you sure it was Bam? There's no way it could be him. He's a secret pooper."

"He's a what?"

"You know, he's bashful, likes to play hide-and-poop," I said this aloud before realizing how stupid it sounded. "How do you know for sure that it's him? It could be any number of dogs." The total number of dogs running wild in Smithtown are three, with the majority belonging to me. The probabilities the offending canine was from my pack were high, and even higher that it was Bam. Regardless, I wasn't going to make this easy for Walt.

"Your neighbor claims she has photographic evidence, and has posted each incident on Facebook. She's hoping the photos will provoke community support in her favor and would eventually have the dog ejected off the island for good."

"Sorry to hear that, Walt." My lip quivered on the edge of hysteria.

"This isn't a laughing matter. When someone comes to the department with a complaint, I have to take it seriously. The woman was insisting that I do something about your dog."

"What did you tell her?" I asked.

"I suggested she try turning a hose on him."

"Oh, that explains why Bam comes home soaking wet."

If you were to search the word *Ridiculousness* on Wikipedia, I'd have no doubt that Bam would be pictured sleeping on his back with legs jetting out in a Superman pose as an example. For Bam, every day was created for him to pee on whatever he desired and roll on the occasional rotted carcass. Only God knows why I love that disgusting fur-ball.

"You've got nothing to go on. You can't prove it was my dog."

"No. Except for the very clear photos on Facebook, I can't."

"Which could be faked. In which case, I suggest we revisit the subject of the missing girls."

"I'd say no, but there isn't any way to stop you from pursuing the idea," Walter sighed, placing his burger down on the paper wrapper.

"Nope, I don't think there is," I answered, victorious.

"You go first, I'm listening," he said, barely paying attention as I droned on about the house, Camo Man, garbage truck, and Walmart's missing children photos, as my voice escalated with every syllable, especially when mentioning the Gas & Go Mart girl.

"Oh yeah, I heard about you passing out face down on a shopping cart at Walmart."

"Huh? How did you hear about that?"

"I hit the lanes with the store manager every Tuesday night without fail. We bowl a few rounds, drink a couple of beers, and have some laughs. It's a good time."

"You're a real exciting guy, Walt, and popular with the ladies I bet. How do you manage to keep them all at bay?"

Walter ignored my comment. "My bowling buddy gives me a call the moment you enter Walmart's doors, just in case. They have your picture tacked to the bulletin board in the security office."

"No, I didn't know that, and what exactly do you mean by *just in case*?" I was growing hot, and Walter knew it.

I can't believe I fell head first into his trap. "Can we move on to what you know about the Camo Man now?"

"You already seem to know all about the activities taking place at that house. Does Hank know what you're up to?" asked Walter, quick to recognize the mere mention of Hank's name would irritate me, but I refused to let it.

"Walt, all human beings are born ignorant, but one has to work hard to remain stupid. You and I both know something ain't right over at that house, and you drive by it, how many times a day without question? Even a blind monkey can see more than you do."

"I ran his plates. The guy's clean, no serious priors, and holds down a job at the Somerset County Hospital. He can't be all that bad if he's helping out sick people."

"Don't placate me like I'm some kind of moron. I'm aware of his employment. I also know that his name is Gordon Myers and that he'll never qualify for the upstanding citizen of Somerset County award."

"I guess we are done here then."

"No sir, we are not done, not by a long shot."

"That's all I know, Molly."

"I hate to disappoint you, Walt, but applying your brush-off technique won't work." My blood pressure pulsed harder through my neck veins. Walter was holding back information.

He's not telling the truth, well, not the whole truth. I would know more than anyone how often the truth twists into something more comfortable to bear, and that kind of truth belongs to a certain kind of person, one full of cracks and jagged edges. This was Walter's version, not mine, and he was fooling no one.

I was on the verge of trying a different angle, a gentler inquisitorial approach, when a parade of cars entered the lot blasting horns and launching obscenities from the driver's side windows. The commotion distracted me.

"What's that all about?" I asked.

"It's the Sniper," answered Walt.

Over on the other side of the creek, on the outskirts of the small town of Parker, the Sniper resides without running water or electricity by choice. It's rumored his financial resources are generated from a trust fund that's managed by his brother. He drives a small white truck at the constant speed of twenty-five miles an hour, on or off the island. The Sniper's name was legendary in these parts, not for anything special that I'm aware of, except for his habit of screaming *Damn Commies* while spitting on the ATM machine at the Gas & Go Mart. He's frequently contentious, and spits at will, or when provoked. The Sniper, more commonly known as the local Boogeyman, has a reputation that can terrify small children.

Two years ago, the terrible cold winter had iced over the surrounding areas. Some of the locals decided to check in on the

Sniper's wellbeing, and in return for their kindness he pointed a shotgun through the window screaming *Get off my land*. On several occasions, I have had my own run-ins with him at the Gas & Go Mart, and without fail he will spit in my direction.

At the food counter, the Sniper purchased a large Pepsi, then turned around heading our way. Walter and I simultaneously bowed our gaze. If you want to avoid a Sniper spitting, it's best to not look him in the eye.

"Here he comes, quick, cover your food. He might be in a bad mood," I said, and Walter instantly shielded his burger with his hands.

Clutching his Pepsi, the Sniper approached our booth staring dead at me, almost as if he could see through me. He paused, then rerouted his direction and walked away. As soon as the Sniper revised his course, an immense sense of relief came over me.

"That is one scary person," I whispered.

"He sure seems fond of you."

"What happened to him, I mean, how did he end up so schizoid?"

"I don't have the whole story, but I heard he used to be quite a looker back in the day. He was the kind of young man the whole town could admire. After their favorite local boy was shipped off to Vietnam, it made him sort of a hero. He was Navy Seals, special-ops or something to that effect. I'm not sure in what capacity, but some say he was pretty high up in rank."

"Then what happened?"

"It's my understanding that he was responsible for the death of his entire squad. With the situation those boys were in, it just takes a simple error in judgment. Look the wrong way and poof, all your men are dead. Whatever happened, it must have gone south real fast."

"I have a theory. I definitely can see him going over the edge one night and killing them all. He's one spooky dude, a bona fide wackadoodle." How insensitive it was of me making outrageous assumptions when I didn't know anything about the guy. But the strange vibe the Sniper was giving us said otherwise.

"Sorry, my mouth has a mind of its own. Go on, finish what you were saying, Walt."

Walter lowered his voice, leaned in closer and spoke. "I also heard he did a stint in the pokey after the incident that killed his men. They say he led them right into the line of fire, but it's hearsay. You know how it is, town talk around here travels faster than a speeding bullet."

"Unfortunately, I've been on the receiving end more often than I care to count," I replied, brutally aware the local talent's ability to fabricate facts about any given person. For the most part, I find the allegations made about me sound a lot more exciting than who I really am.

"He was the sole survivor of the attack and never could forgive himself for not dying alongside his men."

"Sad tale. Local boy does good then does bad. Do you know his real name?" I asked, probing a bit further.

"Sure, it's Sam, Samuel Harris. During the Vietnam war, all the men witnessed or suffered unspeakable acts. Sam wasn't exempt from the horror. He'll never recover from the experience." Walter lowered his gaze. "And now he's considered to be just another ex-military nut-bag. This is what he gets for serving his country."

"The man doesn't deserve to live like he does."

"I remember metal bracelets inscribed with soldier's names on the band," Walter mentioned, his thoughts apparently drifting a bit. "Prisoner of War bracelets."

"Yes, my sister owned one. She never took the thing off until they brought all the soldiers home."

Walter glanced at his watch, then stood, brushing the remainder of his lunch from his Sheriff's uniform. "I think that's enough for today. I have to issue a handful of summonses before four o'clock. Keep your distance from that house Molly, you don't know what kind of mess you could be getting into."

"What do you mean? You can't go now, this just got interesting. Aw, come on, stay five more minutes. I'll spring for a hot apple pie turnover." Grasping at straws, I'd do anything to make Walt stay and give up the information I knew he was holding back.

"Duty calls."

"Please?" I tried my best to smile though he wasn't buying it. My attempt at sounding nice had a nauseating quality to it, like a sickening-sweet cake icing.

"Got to run."

"Pretty please," I whined with eyebrows tweaked on high.

"Throw in a coffee, black with a packet of artificial sweetener. I've been watching what I eat."

Watching it go in your mouth was the zinger I wanted to say but decided against it. "Deal."

I hurried over to the counter, ordered Walter's coffee, and two artery clogging apple turnovers for good measure, then added two cheeseburgers from the dollar menu for the dogs. Since Sara Jane had reached her senior years, I gave her whatever she wanted to eat, which was normally a vanilla soft serve ice cream cone. Today she would have to make do with the burger.

"Your total will be twelve dollars and seventy-eight cents," the counter server said, then handed over the bag filled with greasy fast-food treats. I noticed the server's skin was olive-complected, and he had dark brown eyes with even darker hair descending from a Greek or Italian heritage. Very tall, in his early twenties, and judging by his muscular physique, I'd peg him as a regular at the Total Workout Gym.

As I reached for the food, he pulled back on the bag and said, "Have you ever considered making better food choices?"

"Excuse me?" I handed him a ten-dollar bill and three singles. "What do you mean by that?"

"It's just that you could be in better shape and a lot healthier if you took care of yourself and tried a little exercising."

"Who do you think you are anyway? You can't speak this way to patrons. Where's the manager? I'm not putting up with this."

"I was just making a suggestion," he offered.

"Suggestion my ass. You should take a good look in the mirror bud, Mr. No-neck muscle-bound dweeb. I bet you still live with your mommy, and she still cooks your food and washes your undies. Typical dumb-ass-jock. Why don't you mind your own business and resume your coma-inducing minimum wage job." I felt my neck veins bulge, pulsating at a heart-imploding rate.

Here I go again. I shouldn't let him get under my skin so easily. When incensed, tested, or even slightly annoyed, my mouth has a tendency to fire with a deadly accurate trajectory.

It's the boy's fault. He agitated me. Let's face it, the boy had a crappy job and most likely had a crappy boss who berated him hourly. It wouldn't kill me to stop being such a sphincter. I took a deep breath readying myself for what was unnatural for my character to perform. "Dude, I'm sorry," I apologized like I meant it.

The boy's body stiffened, his face reddened, and his eyes welled up in tears. "You are a very mean person, and you totally suck as a human."

"I'm sorry, what can I do?" He was right. I could have used a friendlier approach, though I never do. Neither did the boy. He was lucky I didn't punch him in the tit for the insult.

The way I see it, we're even.

"If you are truly sorry, you would find a way to make amends," he said.

"How?" I asked.

"You could pay me in cash. Consider it compensation for your personality."

"Aw you know not, that's just plain wrong." I reached in my pocket and drew out the remaining contents, laying one dollar and twenty-three cents, plus the half empty pack of Juicy Fruit Gum on the counter. "That's all I have left. You can have it. It's America's favorite gum after all," I said, beaming a fake smile.

"I don't chew gum. It's bad for your teeth."

"Of course, you don't," I snarled, snatching up the gum and my sack of bad food choices, then returned to our table debating whether I should just go home and start the day over.

"Here, I got an extra pie for you," I said, placing the enticing assortment down before Walter's hungry eyes. I was thankful he didn't witness my ugly display at the counter.

"Thanks," he mumbled, diving straight into a pie.

"Your turn," I said leaning back in the booth.

"You already know I am not allowed to share official police information with non-department personnel, and yet you pester me anyway."

"Why don't you try to view it as enlightening me instead."

Walter let out a sigh. "Whatever I say has to be completely off the record, and it also needs to be off your dinner table conversation with your husband. That last insane round of exploits you pulled almost did him in, and you as well. He can't know about this, understand?"

I rolled my eyes clear around my skull. Walter, disregarding the gesture, scarfed down the second pie. He was right. I do wreak havoc on my friends, my marriage and worse. I frequently scare my husband half to death. Lord knows he doesn't deserve it. I know that I'm responsible for Hank's premature graying along his temples. Last fall when I was kayaking, a sudden onslaught of waterspouts cropped up over the sound. I escaped a direct hit by sheltering in an old hunting cabin on Piney Island that resulted in a two day stay at Somerset County Hospital after falling through the rotted floor. Even though it was just a few stitches and a minor concussion, it worried my husband to no end.

"You make a valid point Walt, and it matches the one on top of your head," I said, quickly regretting not keeping my mouth shut. "Sorry, automatic reaction. Please continue."

"You're wasting energy worrying about that Gas & Go Mart girl. Young people are in a perpetual state of discontent triggered by their raging pubescent hormones. Parents don't kick their children out of the nest in the same way most other animals do. It's just a normal response when a teen rebels. Nature's way of young folk testing their wings in preparation for the real world. The parents can't help but overreact to little Johnny rearing his ugly hormonal head. The tighter the parental clamp, the more he retaliates. It's a vicious cycle."

"I understand what you're saying," I said, thinking of Megan. It's a mystery to me how my parents dealt with my sister throughout her trying teenage years without drinking massive amounts of alcohol to cope. The burden of worry is the penitence paid by all parents bearing children.

"More often than not, the kids come back home on their own accord, tired and hungry, but with an attitude adjustment. But there are those few who go off and start a life clear across the country. That sounds like your Gas & Go Mart girl to me."

"Yes, it sure does. I wish I could have helped her."

"Thousands of children disappear every day, most of them are runaways. But here's the good news, the percentage of unrecovered children is quite low. The worst-case-scenarios are the cases that end badly, by the kid's own doing, or by someone else's hand, and that's the saddest statistic of all. Living on the street is a tough life for any adult to bear, but for the underaged it's deadly. Too often they end up lying on a cold morgue slab from a drug overdose." Walter paused, sipping his coffee for several tedious moments, then signaled for me to move in closer. I was certain he was about to hand me the secret to the universe.

"Molly?" he said in a hushed voice.

"Yes?" I leaned in, eyes and mouth open.

"Are you trying to catch flies?"

"Sorry." I closed my mouth.

"I need you to do something for me."

"Yes, yes, anything, just tell me." This was it, the answer I had been waiting for. The mother-load of Holy Grails in the universe had finally come my way. Surely, the tide had turned in my favor, and I would finally rid the rising mound of maddening crap from my head once and for all and regain my stride. "Go on Walt, tell me."

"Swear to me that you will forget about this and let the authorities do their job, if there even is one to do." With that, Walter gathered his trash from the table, pitched it in the bin, and started for the exit door saying, "Stay clear of that house," and then he left.

"Like that would ever happen," I grumbled, then presented Walter with the special-finger salute I keep reserved for those who irritate me. I couldn't stand the idea of Walter making sense, or that I could actually be wrong about sinister activities fermenting in that creepy house. Even though my intuition screamed otherwise, I had to face the possibility that Camo Man Myers could be just the regular run-of-the-mill weirdo. The only plausible answer I could come up with is that Mr. Sheriff Fat-Man had fooled me. Deep down in my gut I knew Myers wasn't just some ordinary guy. I checked my phone. No new messages. I gazed around the room and saw the snotty server giving me the evil eye and decided to vacate the restaurant before he called me into the authorities for loitering.

-*seventeen*-

Returning to my van, I treated Bam to a hamburger, saving the other one for Sara Jane, then drove the long route home along the tidal creek to avoid passing by the creepy house again. I turned on the satellite radio, switching the news station over to the bluegrass music channel and let the high-lonesome melody calm the stressed areas of my mind. I knew the genre was often considered cornball music, but I found the plum-pitiful lyrics about hardship and heartache rather soothing to my soul.

Rolling into home base, the sunset blazed orange between the graveyard pine trees. The smell of wood stove smoke moved heavily through the chilly air. The burnt odor seeps into our house, drenching every room. When the wind hits an old eastern shore home like ours, it doesn't flow around it like a big rock in the creek, it blows right on through the clapboard without slowing down.

After wasting most of the day I still managed to reach home before Hank and have coffee waiting before he waltzed through the door. Though the coffee was a small gesture, it helped to transition Hank's mental state away from his workday. And he appreciates me without any huge effort on my part.

Sara Jane was always the first to hear Hank's truck pass through the marsh and over the first bridge. The winters are hard on Hank, leaving at first light and returning in the dark dusky hour. He's in perpetual exhaustion; the fallout from both his jobs.

I could tell today was no different when he came through the door.

"Hi Hon, your coffee's ready," I said, sounding upbeat.

"Great," Hank eased himself into the kitchen table chair with shoulders bent under the weight of the day. He slumped over the table looking like a flattened throw pillow. Every year I wonder how much longer he'll last at this pace, but I would never say it aloud, at risk of offending his manhood.

"Long day again?" I asked, setting his mug of hot coffee mixed with three spoons of sugar and a splash of milk down in front of him.

"Yes, grueling. Looking forward to the Christmas party tonight. What about you? How was your day?" Hank rubbed his face.

"You'll never guess."

"I'm beat, please don't make me guess. I don't have the energy."

"I saw an otter by the first bridge, and I ran into Walt at the fast-food joint," I added in case butt-face Walter blabbed to my husband the moment he was out the restaurant door. I figured mentioning the otter sighting would reroute our conversation. The misdirection technique works like a charm on my husband.

"I come across the otters most mornings on my drive into work. They leave a wide wet patch on the road. So, what has old Walt been busy with, besides lunch?"

"Nothing, from what I could tell," I answered. "What about you, got any new stories to entertain me with?" In addition to being extremely talented with the touch of his hand, Hank's also gifted in the art of storytelling.

"Not really, other than a couple of watermen were arrested in Walmart for fighting." Hank drained his cup, then refilled it with the remaining coffee in the pot.

"How did you find out about this?" It's amazing to me how Hank falls onto all the local scuttlebutt that's fit to print before I ever get wind of it.

"Any infraction of the law involving a waterman eventually trickles down the Department of Natural Resource Police wire, and also Walt keeps me posted." Everyone knows Somerset County runs on fried crabcakes and gossip, and Walter held a tight grip at the helm.

"Walt couldn't keep his trap shut if you held a gun to his head," I said. "At least it's good to know I'm not the only person who has problems at that store." I felt vindicated. No longer would I reign as the public idiot. Ah, the sweet taste of victory.

"Molly, you don't have problems, you create them," Hank belly laughed and just like that, my triumph vanished into thin air.

What's for dinner?" asked Hank, his attention switched, zoning in on food.

"Dinner?" I had nothing planned. I forget about those things like cooking, laundry, and generally being thoughtful. "It's nothing fancy," I added, ferreting through the canned goods in the cabinet and began heating up an extra-large can of tomato soup on the gas stove. I pulled out the loaf of white bread, buttering several slices for a grilled cheese sandwich.

"No matter, I'll eat at the party later." Hank remarked, then rubbed his face again. I noticed his restless demeanor, preoccupied by a difficult day he couldn't let go. The department job requires Hank to take action on various wildlife calls rescuing distressed critters, or fetch those trapped in attics and drainpipes. This type of work had left my husband testing positive for the rabies virus, which the Health Department keeps a close eye on by screening his virus levels. Hank assures me he's fit as a fiddle, and that it's safe to live with a small amount of the virus in your system. I guess it's alright, as long as he doesn't bite me.

"I forgot about that party"

"On purpose, I'm sure." Hank turned on the small kitchen television, thumbing the remote until he found the six o'clock news. I find it incredibly rude during our dinner hour, but never protest since I never make anything that would qualify as dinner.

In the background, the television squelched out the same tired programming beginning with political news, followed by community news, then ending with another drug bust in Somerville. Perhaps I make bad food choices, but Hank definitely makes terrible television choices. I wish there was a TV Addiction Anonymous meeting that would help him kick his trying habit.

Hank mumbled a few words in reference to the news, but I didn't hear a word he said over the clatter in my head. I began to wonder about the Gas & Go Mart girl's motivation for messing around with Camo Myers to begin with, and it made my brain hurt. I lowered my head in my hands, blocking the racket in my ears. Hank reached to caress my hand, sending a warm sensation throughout my body and soul, and just like that, all went quiet again.

-eighteen–

"Your boredom is showing," Hank whispered.

"Did I ever tell you how much I hate parties?" I grunted my response.

"At least sixty-four times. You've more than clear about your aversion to social gatherings" he retorted.

"Good. I am glad you understand, and no further explanation is needed." It's not that I'm against celebrating Christmas, I despise all parties equally. I can't be nice for more than an hour and end up drinking too much to cope. At any rate, nobody will have an opportunity to comment negatively about my alcohol consumption tonight because the guest appeared to be considerably more hammered than me, and the party just started.

"Relax, this won't hurt one bit," Hank responded, unfettered by my sarcasm.

"You sound like my dentist."

"Try and enjoy yourself."

"That's not a realistic option. At least my dentist gives me nitrous oxide for the pain."

"There's an open bar."

"Yes, there is that."

"Smile sweetheart, it's only temporary." Hank slid his arm around my waist. He placed his lips near my ear and the hair on my arms responded in light tingles traveling all the way down my body, pre-heating my lady-oven.

"You don't play fair."

"You will be just fine," he said.

"It doesn't seem that way to me."

"Nobody dies from boredom; it just feels that way," he whispered into my neck, setting my nipples on high alert.

"Hmm, the party just got interesting. Can we go home now?" I pleaded.

"Look around you, everyone seems happy," Hank said as he waved hello to a couple making their grand entrance, acting as if they were royalty.

"They're too hoity-toity for my taste. I never bothered to commit their names to memory."

"Can you try and be nice for once?"

"And this is why I hate parties. You have to be nice to people you don't like in the first place. I don't even know half of the people in this room. It feels like we've already been here for an eternity. Do we really need to stay any longer?" I heard the whine in my voice, and it wasn't of the Chardonnay kind.

"We can't leave yet, we just got here. Besides, you look wonderful tonight," Hank smiled with a grin that could make my clothes fall off on their own volition.

Hank tugged on my arm, "Come on, let's go join the offensive people."

"No thanks," I resisted and made a beeline for the punch bowl, shoving a crystal glass into the bright red liquid, almost knocking an ice-burg sized mound of raspberry sherbet over the bowl's edge. "This better be spiked," I grumbled, swallowing a big gulp of foamy sugar. Relieved the liquid contained alcohol, I filled a second glass of the holiday spirit punch. Scanning the party, I caught a glimpse of my reflection illuminated by tiny white lights wrapped around a mirror mounted on the opposite wall. Hank was right, I didn't look half bad squeezed into my low-cut black cocktail dress with a built-in high-rise brazier. Even my hair was behaving properly. Normally I look more like the bride of Frankenstein as the day goes on. It's not that I don't care about my appearance, it's just that I become so engrossed in other projects that I often forget to perform basic personal hygiene like brushing my teeth. The hours sure fly by when you're busy doing nothing of vast importance.

I stared at my husband's face as he glided naturally from one conversation to the next. Working in harsh elements had begun to make its mark, chiseling his sharp edges to a more striking feature by the minute, as I grew more annoying with every passing second.

Hank said something that turned the conversation into laughter.

No wonder everybody adores him. He's entertaining, attractive, skilled in social graces and comfortable in a soiree setting. I find the whole party idea to be an unnecessary ordeal and would rather be home watching a golf marathon on the sports channel with my eyes duct-taped wide open, than to be here.

The doorbell rang out, announcing that additional guests had arrived. I turned to see my beacon of light enter through the door. All hope renewed in my surviving this miserable event.

"About time you got here. You know that making nice was very painful for me," I harped at Julia.

"Sorry I'm late, held up by traffic slowing to glance at a dog lying dead on the side of the road. It must have been hit by a car. Sad for its family to lose their companion."

"That's depressing. Poor little thing. I hate to see critters smashed in the road, but a dog killed by a car is a downright tragic sight."

"I heard the Pope say that all dogs can go to heaven now."

"Oh yeah, that's right, you're Catholic, aren't you?" I smiled.

"Don't you mean a recovering Catholic?" Julia corrected.

"Did I ever tell you about the time when I was driving and a squirrel landed on my windshield?"

"Was he hurt?"

"Other than being scared to death he was fine, although he did show signs of shock after falling from the electric wire onto a moving car. He was looking at me through the windshield, the strangest thing ever."

"Why is it that weird things only happen to you, my dear," Julia laughed, glancing around the room. "Boy, this is some soiree."

"We can sneak out and no one would know," I said desperately as more guests crammed the room with screechy laughter fueled by holiday punch. The music volume set on high maintained the atmosphere until the topic of a specific girl's disappearance came up in conversation. Someone turned down the music and the mood morphed into a sobering heaviness. Voices hushed and attention turned to the subject at hand.

"Seems as though everybody received the same Amber Alerts as you," noted Julia.

"Yeah, it sure sounds that way."

"I have alerts pinging my phone just about every day, but this one had caught me off guard." Julia's fear was founded in reality. In her hometown of Baltimore, there were numerous missing persons, robberies, murders, and other crimes reported on a daily basis. Maintaining a certain amount of complacency towards corruption was vital to self-preservation. It's easier to turn a blind eye than to accept the horrors. But in a town like Fairview, where the total population amounted to two-hundred and eighty-seven, chances are you knew the victim and the person who committed the crime. Six girls were reported missing in Somerset County, with one of them we all knew as the Widow Stone's granddaughter. Her disappearance proved that no matter where you live, evil lurked around every corner in every neighborhood waiting for the perfect moment to raise its ugly head.

"What a tragedy, such a sweet girl," one woman was saying with heart-felt endearment. "After Mrs. Stone's husband passed away, the granddaughter was all she had left in this world. Mrs. Stone looked after that kid like she was her first born. If something awful happened to Rebecca, I just don't see how she would endure."

I noticed the majority of the guests seemed familiar with the Stone family. I didn't even know the girl's name.

"Our church organized a prayer circle," another woman added through a forced cheery lilt.

Clearing his throat, a slightly stout man in a dated tweed jacket appointed himself as the next to speak in authority on the subject of Rebecca Stone. "The last I saw of Becky was when she went door-to-door peddling gift-wrapping paper to fund her school trip. Italy, I think it was. She mentioned something about being a member of the foreign language club that met after school on Wednesdays. Nice girl." The man swirled ice cubes in a glass tumbler, dispensed three fingers of whiskey, then swallowed the contents before resuming his commentary. "There's no denying that what happened to this community is a travesty. Despite the summer insects, this used to be a quiet, civilized place to live. I'm not so sure I feel that way anymore."

I noticed an awkwardness filling the air as people turned their eyes away from the man while he rambled on about their new reality. The only truth they had ever known had been ripped out from under them with no place to land.

The man poured another large glass of merriment on the rocks, then raised his glass, "To Becky's safe and expedient return," then downed the liquor in one gulp.

"Excuse me," I asked, approaching the man. "I'm afraid I didn't know Becky that well. Can you tell me if she was thin and had long blonde hair?" I held my breath, waiting to hear his answer. Either way, a yes or no response would mean the same outcome for the Gas & Go Mart girl. She was somewhere out there in the world, and most likely in serious danger.

The man waited a moment for the whiskey to stabilize his reasoning before answering. "Why no, she's not blond at all. Her hair is darker, thick and wavy. Becky was pudgy around her middle like me. Mrs. Stone makes the best cakes this side of the Bay Bridge," he said, patting his belly.

"Thank you, I must be thinking about someone else then."

"Quite alright," he said, then resumed pursuing a hard whiskey buzz.

On the side of the room, someone began singing a Christmas Carol, prompting others to join in and the jolly timbre of the party gradually returned. I searched for my husband and saw Hank perusing the buffet table, piling his plate into a high colorful mound of food. On the other side of the room, Julia, who was holding court with several other people about who-knows-what, appeared to be enjoying herself. I didn't want to spoil her fun and decided to meander amongst the crowd eavesdropping for entertainment before my boredom could kick back in. My satisfaction came directly.

"It's my understanding, the Meals on Wheels van had trouble delivering food to his house, and that he was fairly belligerent about the presence of the agency on his property," said a woman draped in gaudy costume jewelry who was having a word with Walter. Gauging by his body language, she was standing a bit too close for his comfort.

"Who are we talking about?" I asked, deliberately interrupting their conversation. The woman in turn gave me a dirty look, then repositioned her body to block my access.

"Oh, don't you worry honey, he's all yours for the taking," I laughed.

Oblivious to our snitty exchange, Walter carried on as if I wasn't there. "Yes, that's correct. His food is now being delivered by a state police escort. The trooper immediately impounded all of the man's firearms so he won't be taking pot-shots at volunteers anymore," Walter said, eating from a paper plate bulging with appetizers bound to add a few pounds to his midsection. "I'm the designated escort tomorrow since the majority of state police units will be patrolling traffic up at the Holiday Spirit parade in Somerville."

"Who are you talking about?" Finally, the party held some fascination for me.

"The Sniper," Walter snapped, and shot me a look hard enough it could have knocked me over. It didn't faze me. With my attention rekindled, I pushed past the woman grabbing Walter by the elbow and drug him behind the Christmas tree, knocking several ornaments crashing to the floor.

"What now Molly? Look at that, you made a crab-puff fall on the floor, and it was the last one too."

"Shush, lower your voice please, I don't want Hank to hear us, he might get suspicious."

"Molly, look at us. We're hiding behind a pine tree decorated with enough lights to guide a seven-forty-seven jet plane down a runway in a dense fog. The whole world can see you and me. Come on, let me go. You're going to make me miss out on the rest of the hors d'oeuvres. And there's something painfully pointy that's sticking me in the backside."

"No, you answer me first, and then I'll let you go. Do you feel the Sniper could have had something to do with any of the disappearances?"

"What makes you think that he's responsible?"

"Because he's ex-military and acts as kooky as a cartoon Looney Tune, that's why."

"That's just ridiculous."

"I'm going out to his house with you tomorrow."

Walter took a deep breath as if he was going to let me have it, but instead shook his head in defeat.

"Arguing with you will get me nowhere fast. I can't believe I am going to say this," he paused, "meet me in the morning at the old Gino's store at eight o'clock sharp. You can follow me out to the Sniper's place. I know you'll go ahead and make the trip without me, and you shouldn't go anywhere near there by yourself."

"Trust me, I have reservations about going there by myself as well. Wait a minute, you did say that the police took away all of his guns, right?"

"Yes, yes, they are good as gone," Walter confirmed.

"Good, it would be hard explaining to my husband why there was a gaping hole in my chest."

"The authorities relieved Sam of his guns last month, I thought you were eavesdropping on our conversation. Now that you have what you want from me, why don't you go over with Hank and make nice to people?"

"No need, he's coming our way. Not a word said about this, okay?" I pleaded through crinkled eyebrows.

"Keeping Hank in the dark never ends well," Walter countered in a whisper.

Eyeing us both, Hank made his way to the tree with hands on hips. "What are you two knuckleheads doing? If I didn't know any better, I'd say you were making a pass at my wife, Walt."

"I'm going to volunteer, like you said I should. I'm helping Walt with his Meals on Wheels route tomorrow," I stated, sounding grateful. Landing on my feet like a cat had always been one of my worthier attributes.

Hank glared at both of us. "Uh huh, I just bet you are. In any case, you'll be protected by the counties' finest." He reached out, wrenching me loose from behind the Christmas tree. Walter seized the opportunity and hoofed it to the buffet.

"Did I mention how amazing you look in that dress? Why don't we go someplace where I can help you slip out of it?"

"Are you sure it's not the bourbon doing the talking?" I asked, aware I'd be the one driving us home tonight.

"What do you think?" Hank purred into my hair then discretely ran his finger outlining my breast and I gasped. His lips hummed a vibrating shock-wave, electrifying my lady accouterments.

"The sooner the better," I grinned.

-nineteen-

Readying myself for the day ahead, I slammed a second cup of coffee burning down my throat, then pummeled my hair into submission with a brush. After a night of marital midnight bedroom gymnastics, my red eyeballs bore proof. I woke exhausted and starving, but didn't want to waste time and miss meeting Walter.

I'm way too riled up to consider nutrition at the moment anyway. I'm certain the trip out to the Sniper's house will score the info I need on the Gas & Go Mart girl. Then, I'll be able to put her, and all the missing women behind me, and finally gain the peace my weary soul desires. And after that, I think I'll put my mind on vacation for a while.

Another text message sounded and my heart sank. Regretting ever having the function installed on my phone, I opened the app to see the text was from Walter saying it was slow driving on frozen roads, and would be at our meeting place a few minutes late. I understood how Walter might be a little apprehensive about this morning's task, with the Sniper's hokey disposition being what it was. My emotions may convey excitement at the prospect of achieving resolution, but at the same time I'm not stupid about the real possibility of having my head blown to smithereens.

I hurried my pace while driving safely off island, watching for sporadic icy patches that had formed overnight across the road. The howling winds coated miles of needle rush in frost. Reeds glistened under the sunlight, moving in a syncopated wave of shimmering light. In Smithtown, the winter was as stunningly breathtaking as it is devastatingly harsh. More than once, I've received an icy wind burn on my face in less than a minute. And as far as I could tell, the current winter season had already exceeded its reputation. I shuddered at the thought of the low temperatures yet to come in our drafty house. Another four months of bundling up in a heavy coat just to stay warm inside the house.

Every winter, the brutal weather freezes over the harbor, trapping the oyster boats in several inches of thick ice, causing the oyster market, along with the watermen, to suffer a financial gale-force-blow. It's incredibly unnerving to see waves freeze mid-motion. Last winter, the east winds blew horrendously for days on end, pushing saltwater up the bay and spilling out onto the roads. When the water finally receded, it left behind in its wake miniature icebergs that were impossible to pass. It was in that same dreadful year, when Hank had rescued a severely distressed great blue heron from the cold. The gangly bird, unable to fish enough nourishment from the frozen creek gut, had become too weak to stand on its own. Hank set the wobbly bird by the wood stove warming his bones. He stayed with the frozen creature through the night, stoking the fire, but come the early morning hour, death had taken the bird. It's incomprehensible how swiftly island elements can take a life without prejudice or remorse. It's just as impossible trying to accept nature's justification for its cruelty. Hank appreciates the earth's order and flows naturally alongside it. They are one in the same, on land or on the water. I admire his natural abilities, his goodness and strength to selflessly act on what was right without thought.

Too bad I'm not half the man my husband is. One of my biggest grievances with old-man-winter is that the fun factor goes AWOL, unless you find freezing your ass off fishing ghost pots during the iciest month of the year to be a good time. Hank sees dragging a net behind the boat searching for lost crab pots as a real hoot. I think it's a drag, period. I'd rather spend the day shoveling chicken manure with a plastic spoon.

I miss the warmer weather and having fun with Hank on Oyster Island. I want to be barefoot and standing very still in the water letting the crabs crawl over my feet. I want to be all alone with my husband in the sunshine, nobody else, just the two of us and the dogs, and maybe some wine.

Pulling into the sandy lot at old Gino's store, I put the van in park and let the engine run. The little bit of warmth leaking through the heater vents was a blessing. I wiped my hand across the steamy windshield, clearing a view to the dilapidated building. The previous owners had long since retired and closed up shop way before I moved here. In its hay day, the store stocked all the essentials needed for shore living: milk and bread, rope, random brass fittings, and the infamous eastern shore white crabbing boots. All that and two small tables set to the side where deli sliced sandwiches were consumed and tall tales were told. The mom-and-pop store was treasured by all the locals. Now everyone had no choice but to drive the half-hour long haul to the mainland just for a quart of milk.

The property fell into serious disrepair years ago, and was now viewed as an eyesore by the community. The years of neglect had taken their toll on the abandoned building. The roof slouched inward, and the store's sign had fallen to the ground, buried under tall grasses. The structure's paint peeled from the stucco plaster, flecking across the lot like freckles on a fair-skinned child in the summertime.

It's a disgrace nobody gave thought to starting up the business again. With a little gumption and a lot of elbow grease, the old Gino's Store could once more be a viable asset to the community.

I checked the hour on my phone. It was unusual for Walter to run late. He would have made allowances for weather delays in his route. Being Mr. Punctual, Walter should have made it by now, unless he was really enjoying a fast-food breakfast.

The idea of Walter eating a hot greasy breakfast started my stomach rumbling from hunger. I searched the car for something to dampen the pangs and found a half-eaten candy bar, plucked the dog hair from the sticky end, and then munched on the stale nugget. Two minutes later, my blood sugar levels were within normal range, and I was able to concentrate on my mission. Speculating about what the Sniper might shed light on, I grew more excited by the minute.

Hearing stones crunching under car tires, I thought Walter had arrived, and peered through the frosted window to see a Jeep Grand Cherokee slowing to a stop. The window slid down.

"How have you been Molly?" asked Clair Conner. I winced. Clair was Fairview's equivalent of a town gossip crier. Nobody can bend the truth into a weapon like Clair, and one must be extra careful not to give her any ammunition.

"I'm fine, Clair, and you?" I asked, wishing she would just leave. But I'm never that lucky.

"What are you doing parked out here all by yourself? Looking for more trouble?" she cackled.

Great, I bet this reaches Hank before his lunch hour and it'll set him off worrying over nothing. Clair's mouth was more dangerous than a loaded shotgun cocked and ready to fire at a moment's notice. Her voracious chin-wagging can generate rumors faster than a speeding bullet. I should know. I've been in her crosshairs on more than one occasion. The woman has no-do-right in her.

"I pulled over to make a phone call," I responded. "It's illegal to talk and drive."

"Well, aren't you a little good-deeder?" Clair rattled on with her lips flapping non-stop about this one and that one, while I kept my eye on the rearview mirror. Finally, I caught a glimpse of Walter round the bend and hauled ass, cutting off the cruiser and leaving Clair behind, completely stunned by my sudden exit.

Walter maintained a close tail on my van as I turned down Parker Road and onto the rutted dirt driveway, bumping over potholes that ended at a structure hidden by dead trees. I shut the engine off, scrutinizing the Sniper's house. Entirely covered in scrub vines, anyone driving by would never know that there was a house behind that overgrowth. Listening to Sniper stories all these years, I knew exactly where his house was located.

Parking the cruiser, Walter gingerly emerged from the vehicle, leaving the keys in the ignition for a quick get-away. Scanning the front windows of the Sniper's house, he stepped around the cruiser mindful of his footing on the sketchy uneven ground. "What was that about back there?" he asked.

"Clair Conner, she's a human wrecking ball," I answered, with a breath visible in the cold condensed air. "Not worth taking a chance of her seeing me get into your car."

"Yes, you're right about that. Small town, small minds." Walter gathered food provisions from the back seat of the cruiser, balancing the items in his arms. "Okay, Molly, are you ready for this?"

"I guess so," I answered, knowing there was a good chance the Sniper might shoot a hole through my forehead.

"Hello, anybody home? It's the Sheriff's Department with your Meals on Wheels delivery," Walter hollered at the house in his professional departmental voice used in hostage situations. It made me uncomfortable.

"Are you sure they took his guns?" I whispered.

"Yeah, I'm pretty sure." Walter wavered a moment, then cautiously continued to move towards the house. I held up the rear, using his round body as a shield. When we reached the house's splintered steps, the front door creaked open the width of a frog's hair, and then wide enough fit the barrel of a shotgun.

"I don't know about this, Walt. This feels weird to me. What if the Sniper had hidden a gun somewhere on the property? What if he has it aimed at us right now?" I was scared, with every reason to be.

"We'll be fine. It's spaghetti day, his favorite. Come on, let's go in and get this over with," Walter said, sliding the door fully open, then walked inside. I did the same, following like a dumb-ass lamb to the slaughter.

"How are we doing today?" Walter inquired with genuine interest, a side of him I'm rarely privy to. To most people, Walter is known as a compassionate man, and commendable in his ways, often following up on evictees to check on their well-being. Over the years, Walter managed to chip away at my psyche, lessening my defenses. Though he may be considered an upstanding guy by those acquainted with him, instinct tells me to maintain my guard at all times.

The Sniper sat at a small table resting his elbows on a red and white checkered tablecloth that could easily hide a shotgun beneath. The man was equally as spooky as his residence. Trying not to stare and agitate the man, I averted my gaze checking out the threadbare interior and sweeping across the warped wooden flooring. In the corner, the Sniper had a small wood stove as his heat source and used a propane camping lantern stationed on the table for lighting.

"Still able to sit up and take nourishment, as you can see," he spoke in a raspy voice, without his usual venomous hatred. In fact, the Sniper's manor was a far cry from how I usually see him behave at the Gas & Go Mart. This man was a meager facsimile, downtrodden and reduced to someone else. This wasn't the

Sniper I knew to be feared by all. He looked up to Walter, then pointed his chin at me.

"This is Molly Hanson, my helper for today." Walter placed the spaghetti dinner package on an empty chair, then removed the used food trays and other trash out to the squad car, leaving me alone with the Sniper.

"I don't care to know who she is, or you for that matter," he scowled out the opened door.

"Is it alright if I ask you a few questions?" I asked, and he cocked his head, raised a befuddled eyebrow and grunted something indecipherable. I understood the gesture to mean that my presence was invading his space. On the upside, he didn't recognize me from the Gas & Go Mart.

"You can ask, don't mean I have to answer you," The Sniper leaned back in his chair, crossing his arms like a pouting child.

"I was hoping you might know something about the recent disappearances, mainly about the widow Stone's granddaughter," I inquired calmly, surprised I found the courage to speak.

The Sniper swung his chair around, scratching the floor, then spoke with his back to me, "You are a very foolish woman. You're a dog chasing her own tail. I know about your kind, I know about a lot of things, and let me tell you, young lady, some of those things you don't want to know anything about."

"Would you have information about the man that lives opposite the Sheriff's Department? I'm sure you've seen him at the Gas & Go Mart. I'm talking about the man who dresses in camo clothing every day?"

"Maybe I do, and then maybe I don't. What would you like to know about him?" he inquired, grinning like a Cheshire cat. "I can tell you he's got no business outfitting himself in military gear. He ain't served a day in his life. And I also know you like poking your nose where it doesn't belong."

I had a hunch this was going to take a while. The Sniper enjoyed toying with me. "Is there something else you know about camo man?" Behind me I heard Walter enter the room, catching my last question.

"Anything you can tell us, Sam, would surely help us out."

"Yes, thank you, Sam, anything at all, even if you feel it isn't important," I added, remembering that old saying about catching more flies with honey. "Several women from our area are reported as missing. The police believe they could be in serious danger. A man with your expertise might know something that could help the authorities locate them."

The Sniper uncrossed his arms and said, "Maybe you're looking in the wrong place. You're not thinking like the enemy, and you'll be running circles until you do. In Vietnam, I started out as a combat infantryman. In war, it doesn't matter how much money you got, or who you are, or where you came from. We were all fighting for our lives. Nobody left that hell-hole with a clean conscience. We were just kids and didn't know what we were doing, but the consequences of our actions will haunt us just the same. All those poor men, so many casualties, it was pointless, all for nothing." The Sniper's voice trailed and his eyes turned vacant as if a switch in his head had shut off. The idea that the Sniper might lose his grip without warning and pull out a gun and murder us both flashed before my eyes. I shot a nervous look at Walter and he motioned the go-ahead towards the door. Every survival fiber in my body screamed to run as fast as I could, but then I heard the Sniper's voice soften and mumble something about his men. "They were my friends, and I lost them all."

"It's alright, Sam. I'll be around tomorrow and check-in to see how you're doing." Walter stepped closer, putting a hand on the Sniper's shoulder as he sobbed into his hands.

When I left the man's house, knowing I was going to live to see another day, my blood pressure dropped within normal limits in seconds. Walter wasn't far behind making it to my van.

"You okay?" he asked, and actually meant it.

"It's terrible the Sniper turned into such a pitiful being," I answered, out of the Sniper's earshot.

"Don't take it personally. He gets like this, upset at the whole world. You bend something far enough it will break, and the war snapped him like a dry twig. Sam's not as scary as everyone thinks he is. I'm sure you're disappointed not finding the answers you came out here for. Hopefully, the trip satisfied your curiosity enough that you'll leave Sam out of your harebrained schemes in the future. That goes for me as well, I can't help you anymore, I'm not legally allowed to."

Walter warmed up the squad car, then bounced over the dirt lane returning to his duties. I left the Sniper's house with the tiniest inkling that I should do more for humanity. I could try random acts of kindness, and then move onto volunteering, or read to the elderly, or I could clean dog pens at the local animal shelter. But all those ideas would have to sit on the back burner. I was still hungry and the stale candy bar only teased my appetite into a ravenous fit. Knowing that several courses of Chinese food would remedy the situation perfectly, I redirected my van and pondered our Sniper visit for the duration of the route towards Somerville.

-twenty-

On the north side of the main highway, stands a short strip-mall where the China Delight Restaurant, the Exxon gas station, and the Suds & Grub pizzeria laundromat combo has met the multiple needs of travelers for decades. It's a fair distance to travel from Smithtown just for a take-out food order, but when starving, it seemed endless.

I pulled into the China Delight parking lot and found an empty spot. I opened the van door and was instantly subdued by air laced in delectable, exotic scents. Inside the restaurant, the aromas intensified and I thought I might pass out in ecstasy. After studying the takeout menu carefully, as if one wrong move would mean certain death, I made my selections.

"Can I help you?" asked a small Asian woman who appeared behind the counter by magic.

"Yes, please, I would like a number twenty-seven, a number thirty-six, two number sevens, a number twelve, plus a spring-roll to go."

The woman quickly marked my order, circling the large array of items from the menu sheet, then disappeared into the kitchen. Shouts erupted over banging pots and frying pans behind the kitchen doors. The commotion sounded as if they were beating each other to a pulp. Within minutes, the woman resurfaced, looking no worse for wear, and handed me a spring-roll secured inside a wax-paper sack.

"Your order will be ready in ten minutes," she said. They always say that.

Waiting for my massive amount of food, I sat down on a bench by the entrance, snacking on complimentary fried noodles smothered in two packets of duck sauce. The room's decorations paired well with melodic tunes playing softly overhead. Though the hour was premature for the dinner rush, I did notice the restaurant was exceptionally quiet and empty, except for a man dressed in business attire dining alone at a table by the window, and a middle-aged couple heavily making out in a booth towards the back. I figured they were married, just not to each other.

It wasn't long before the woman behind the counter yelled, announcing my food was ready, and then proceeded to ring up the order. "Twenty-six fifty-eight please," she said through a toothy smile.

I gave her two twenty-dollar bills, then looked into the enormous bag of food, spying only two fortune cookies, bummer. I'll eat one now and save the other for Hank. I pried open the cookie with my fingernail and read the fortune. *After bad luck comes prosperity.*

With the way my luck rolls I doubt that will ever happen.

I retrieved the second fortune cookie from the bag and stuffed it in my mouth, then unfolded the paper to see what dumb saying this fortune offered.

I am watching you. The words sprang from the scrap of paper, jarring my whole being. The fortune had struck a nerve wide open, allowing my paranoia to run rampant. This had to be some sort of joke. I looked around the dining room, no one was laughing. I felt the blood leave my face as I became dizzy.

"Everything okay?" The cashier asked.

Tucking the food bag into my arms, I rushed out of the restaurant. "All good," I responded over my shoulder.

The woman scrambled around the counter. "Wait, your change, you forgot your money," she hollered at the closing door.

I quickly climbed inside the van and turned the key. Nothing happened, no sparks or rattles. Once more I tried the ignition but the engine was unresponsive. My van had coded and was now heading towards the afterlife. This had happened twice before. I should have had a mechanic look at it like Hank said, but I never did get around to it. I was hoping the problem would just go away on its own.

Because of my van's advancing age, I kept Somerset Towing on speed-dial. Digging the cell phone from my pocket, I called for a tow and was told it would be several hours before they'd pick up my van. I said I would leave the keys under the floor mat. Nobody in their right might would ever think about stealing the van. My next step was rehearsing what to say before making that dreaded phone call to Hank. I took a breath and pressed his number on speed-dial.

"Aw, you know not. Why didn't you get that hunk-of-junk fixed the first time this happened?" Just like I thought, Hank was livid.

"I guess I just forgot and didn't do it."

"Of course, you didn't Molly, and why am I not surprised? You have nothing to do and all day to do it, and yet you still couldn't manage a trip to the repair shop."

"I'm sorry Hank. I'll have it fixed now."

"I have a lot of work left. It will be a while before I can come get you."

"That's fine. I'll take the bus. You can meet me at the repair shop after work."

"You drive me nuts, you know that?" Hank hung up, no goodbye, no nothing.

I crossed over to the north side of the highway to wait at the no-frills bus stop for public transportation to show. I say no frills because it lacked a weather shelter and of course a bench. However, it did contain a sign indicating where losers should stand. To make matters worse, the temperature was falling fast. I yawned, shivering as the bus took its good old sweet time to arrive. I've heard that drowsiness was the first sign of hypothermia. I yawned again, then started dancing in place to keep my blood flowing. Two car horn honks in appreciation for my fabulous footwork later, the bus appeared. The door swished open and a rush of warmth came over me. I managed to find a seat on the crowded vehicle wedging my body next to a very overweight man who surveyed my food bounty with his hungry eye. I tightened my grip on the China Delight.

The bus moved onto the highway, gaining speed until reaching the next stop. The driver hit the brakes with a jolt, nearly inflicting whiplash on all the passengers. The bus sustained its route moving at a painful snail's pace repeating the hard landings and even harder departures. The methodical ride provided ample time to contemplate every nagging issue that filtered into my thought process, including my sister and why I hadn't heard from her for a few days.

I should count my blessings, but when I do, I usually get stymied at number zero.

I sent a text to Megan, asking if she was alright. Despite our differences, and this emotional distrust I retain, there's an inherent aspect in my nature to help people. I tried to conjure every trick that would ease her pain, but all my attempts were in vain. I had to face it. I don't have superpowers to locate the missing, or the girl from the Gas & Go Mart. She could be anywhere in the world by now. It was the truth, plain and simple, and it landed like a cement cinder block between my eyes.

The combination of breathing diesel fumes and the rocking rhythm of the bus made me sleepy and I leaned my head against the window glass. I began to drift and fought to stay awake until there, behind my eyelids, came the image of my mother.

***

"Molly, come on, hurry up. Go get your sister or you will both be late for school." My mother said, alive and well, and standing directly in front of me. I reached out and touched her face and instantly I was six years old riding on the bus to school.

"I have to leave now," she smiled, then kissed and hugged me goodbye.

"When will I see you again?"

"Very soon dear. Your father and I will be right here watching over you."

The school bus door opened and I stepped out into the thin, white air. I turned to the bus driver, who gave me a wink with his sparkling blue eyes as the bus pulled away and I was left standing all alone.

***

The bus's brakes squealed to an abrupt stop, knocking my head against the window.

"Oh no," I gasped, realizing I slept past my bus stop and was now somewhere in the north end in the city of Salisbury. Hank was going to kill me.

One by one, the passengers poured off the bus. My cell phone buzzed. Of course, it was Hank.

"Where are you? I've been here at the office waiting for your call."

"I'm in Salisbury, almost to the terminal. I fell asleep and missed my stop," I said, frantically searching for my huge China Delight bag, but it was nowhere to be seen. "And someone stole our dinner," I added, receiving a silent reply. "It wasn't my fault." More silence. "Hank, are you still there?"

"Stay right where you are. I'm coming to get you." Without another word Hank disconnected. It didn't take a genius to figure out that he was upset with me again.

The bus maintained its slow route. I felt like a big putz and lay my head in my hands to sulk. It's not like I fell asleep on purpose. Rubbing my face, I glanced through my fingers and couldn't believe my eyes. Across the bus aisle sat my jolly hitchhiker staring back at me.

"You shouldn't talk to yourself. People will think you're a lunatic," he said.

"Too late, my reputation is etched in stone. What are you doing here anyway? I thought you were somewhere in Tennessee."

"I was."

The bus pulled into the busy terminal and the last of the passengers hurried off the bus, all except for Santa.

"That doesn't explain what you are doing here in my neck of the woods," I said, convinced my life could not get any weirder at this point, and my growing hunger pangs only fueled the confusion.

"I had many places to visit," he said, jumping up from his seat, then moved towards the bus's exit door. "Got to run, lots to do." He laid his finger to the side of his nose and winked, then disappeared into the crowded sea of people.

"Wait," I cried, but he was gone in a flash. I stepped down the bus steps to see Hank waiting at the bottom with arms folded. "Did you see him? Which direction did he go?" I asked.

"Who are you talking about? I didn't see anyone get off the bus but you."

"Santa, the guy I picked up hitching a ride was supposed to be in Tennessee."

Hank smacked his forehead, turned and stomped towards the terminal parking garage. I followed behind knowing this was going to be another very long ride home.

"I'm sorry you had to drive all the way up here. I fell asleep. I had a long, tiring day that began early in the morning with Walt. We went to the Sniper's house to find out what he knew about the recent disappearances, but the Sniper inquisition turned out to be a bust. However, it hasn't removed Camo Man from my suspect list. And then my van broke down, and I had to take the bus, and then when I dozed off someone had stolen my China Delight bag. And to top it off I saw Santa Claus riding the bus!" Hearing my ridiculous voice blather on I was certain my next stop would be the hospital psych ward. I've often thought that if I hurled myself off the end of the pier it would wash away all my craziness and make my world normal like everyone else.

"Walt? You mean to tell me you dragged Walt into our mess?" Hank cupped his hands over his forehead, and for a brief second, I thought I saw steam rise.

"But you don't understand, Hank. You don't know the fortune cookie said that someone was watching me. Not to mention that Santa guy, I mean what are the chances of running into him again?" I asked, my words now defensive.

"Molly, when will you recognize the enormity of your actions? When will you ever be satisfied and stop wanting more, and more? When Molly, when?"

Hank was mad. I knew what would fix this. Once more I drew out my Juicy Fruit gum, counted only three sticks left in the pack, then debated if I felt like sharing.

"Piece of gum?"

"No," Hank snapped.

"Good, all the more for me then," I said, tossing a stick in my mouth. The gum hadn't worked its magic on Hank. I didn't know what else to do. I sank into the seat, chalking this day up as another on my long list of regrets, like the time I flew dressed as a nun just to gain preferential seating on the plane. Hopefully, I still have time to fix that one with God.

Hank refused to speak for what seemed like thousands of painful miles. And after arriving at the house, he marched inside and slammed the door behind him and went straight upstairs to bed without eating supper or kissing me goodnight. I also stomped inside the house but chose to head straight for the wine instead, pouring an ample amount into a glass.

Picking up on the tension in the air, the dogs huddled on the kitchen floor. I tried placating them both with dog cookies, and then proceeded to ply myself with the large glass of wine in hopes it would be enough to knock me out for the entire night.

Upstairs, I didn't bother stripping off my clothing before quietly sliding in the bed next to Hank. He rolled over, taking the covers with him. I lay there staring at the wooden sign hanging on the far bedroom wall that read, *Always kiss me goodnight,* a wedding present given to us by dear friends. I thought about our nuptials performed by the water on a beautiful insect-free September day. I remembered Hank wore his white crabbing boots as I thought he was the most stunning creature I've ever seen.

I never meant to bring my very tolerant husband to anger, but somehow, I always do. "I'm sorry," I spoke faintly, fighting a tear forming in the corner of my eye.

Hank repositioned his body and placed his hand on my arm and whispered, "Everything is going to be okay."

"I'm sure you're right." I answered, doubtful that would ever happen in my lifetime.

-*twenty-one*-

"Do you need a lift?" It was Julia ringing my cell at seven thirty-five in the morning. "I'm leaving for Baltimore and need to take off soon before the clog of weekenders get on the road or it will take an extra four hours to get home. I could drop you off at the repair shop. It's on my way."

"Huh?" I mumbled half awake.

"I tried your cell earlier, but it went straight to voicemail."

"I left it plugged in the charger all night. I didn't plan on speaking to anyone this early."

"If you want a ride, we have to leave the island shortly."

"Yes, thank you. The repair shop said the van would be ready later this morning. I can't wait all day for Hank to take me. You know what happens when I'm held against my will on the island."

"I'm afraid I do," Julia agreed.

Normally, I would take offense, but waiting for Hank was definitely out of the question.

"Wait a minute, how did you hear about my van?"

"The Smithtown news wire, evening gossip edition," she replied. I could hear the smirk in her voice. Julia was right. I make the headlines more often than not. When it pertains to my relationship with local gossip, I'm afraid my mishaps are all I'll be remembered for.

"I just need a few minutes."

"I'm ready when you are," Julia announced. Her stay on the island was short. I knew I wouldn't see her again until the white egrets return in the spring, and would miss her company. Hank is usually too busy, or too tired to deal with me. I'm not complaining, I know he works very hard for the both of us. It's Julia's friendship that keeps me sane. Also the wine helps.

With my coat on and a cup of coffee in hand, I waited at the front door until Julia turned onto our oyster shell driveway with her car packed to the gills. Julia moved her bags to the back seat, steadying it on top of the rest of the already piled high mound and blocking her rear-view visibility.

"You have room to sit now."

"Thank you. I was starting to grow mold waiting for you," I said getting into the passenger's seat and fastened my seatbelt.

"Ah, that would explain your attire."

"Very funny. You're going to be lonely in Baltimore without me."

"Yes, it will be tough going without your misadventures. Though I must say I won't miss the terrible winds, or the constant cold on my feet." Julia cranked up the temperature, a soothing warm air eased through the vents. "Don't worry, I'll be back before you know it, kiddo."

"This means I'll have to drink wine all alone. How sad is that?" I asked. It was true. I was not looking forward to the next couple of months turning a deeper shade of diluted gray. It's downright depressing. No matter the weather, Julia always turns the day into sunny skies.

"Hey, do you need to stop at the store?" she asked, slowing the engine as we passed by the Gas & Go Mart.

"No, I'm good, thanks," I replied, though it was far from the truth because much like Julia's car, I was overloaded from the hitchhiking girl sitting in the backseat of my mind. I couldn't set one foot on the store's premises and expected to sleep the remainder of the year.

Rounding the corner onto the connecting road to route thirteen, we passed by the sheriff's office averting our eyes as if it were never there.

"What's with the parade of traffic? Can you see anything up ahead?" Julia strained her neck past the line of cars stretching almost to the highway entrance. She brought her car to an idling stop.

"No, I can't see what the holdup is, but I can hear it."

As vehicles began to peel away, the sound grew in intensity the nearer we came to the cause. Stemming from the massive truck, metal band music punched the air waves, pulsating inside Julia's car.

"I think my ears are bleeding," said Julia, her car now caught behind the county's garbage truck haphazardly parked at the creepy house, blocking both lanes with no way of moving around it.

"I told you. It's the same scene repeating right before our eyes," I said, frantically pointing at the camo dude as he handed over a package to the driver. Stuck behind the stinky truck, we had the perfect view as Camo Man got into his station wagon and pulled out ahead of the trash truck.

"Yes, it certainly appears peculiar," she replied, as baffled as I was about it. "The transaction gives the impression it's something illegal, but we really don't know the whole situation." Julia, unwilling to engage any further in my conspiracy theories, or take the risk of inciting another escapade, chose her words carefully. Her only desire was to return to city civilization with its off-Broadway plays and its four-star restaurants. I didn't blame her for feeling that way.

"How can you say that after seeing what went down between the two of them?" I asked without taking my eyes off the truck.

"Yes, it's true that I just saw one man hand another man an envelope. But that's all I saw."

"I bet there's a huge load of money in that envelope."

"Probably there is," Julia admitted after seeing the transaction. This meant I had proof I wasn't crazy after all.

"Park there," I said pointing to the curb.

"Why?"

"I'm going to find out what sort of weirdness Myers may be up to in his creepy house, and you're coming with me."

"No way Molly, I am not going with you. Besides being dangerous it's insane, not to mention the trespassing issue. How can I say this so you will understand?" Julia began to mouth her words in slow motion, "No way, no how am I getting involved in another one of your foolish antics in any way, shape, or form."

"Why not? We'll be fine. The guy left the house. Nobody's home. We'll just be having a look around, that's all. Pull over and park right here, we won't be long," I said, confident in my plan.

"I don't like this idea one bit." Julia reluctantly moved her new car over to the side of the road, parking in the same spot across from the sheriff's department as before but in broad daylight. Anyone could spot us.

"Look here Molly, I'm still not over our run in with Walt. And as I recall, the last big scheme you drug me into we almost had the Department of Natural Resource Police aiming their guns at us. I thought we were goners for sure."

"Yes, that was a bit of a surprise, eh?" I asked. "Good times."

"Good times my ass. My heart was pounding so hard I thought it would explode into pieces."

"There's nothing like a near death experience to let you know you're still alive." It was beyond my understanding how Julia could still be harboring ill will over a silly misunderstanding that occurred long ago when we stumbled upon a sting operation while kayaking and ruined NRP's raid.

If Julia can't bring herself to forgive me, then I have no choice but to disregard her feelings.

"You coming or what?" I asked, exiting the car. Julia grudgingly followed.

"I still don't like this one bit."

"But you find it intriguing. Deep down inside there's a sense of excitement."

"Yes, maybe there is that," Julia answered, fighting a developing smile.

"See, you're going to miss me."

"I suppose I will, for a little while."

"Then walk this way."

We padded around to the backside of the house, cautious of the rusting metal parts wedged in every nook and cranny available. I found angling around the debris much easier in the daylight.

"Wow, there sure is a lot of junk back here. What is all this stuff?" asked Julia.

"Look over here," I motioned beyond the scrubby bushes growing alongside the house. "That's where the door should be located, the one I told you about." I spoke with an air of confidence. Seeing the property completely different in the light of day felt less intimidating. The place was a dump, day or night.

"What do you suppose that is?" asked Julia. On the farthest end of the field stood a structure under mature oak trees. "It looks pretty rough."

"How odd, I don't recall seeing the building that night. I think it's some sort of barn, probably for storing equipment. We should check it out," I said, stepping high over frozen grasses in the direction of the building.

Nearing the barn, the mismatched planks of wood used in construction became clearly noticeable. "I'd assume someone built this by hand with scrap wood," I said to Julia, but didn't hear her feet crunching over the frozen ground. She had stopped moving about ten feet back. "What's the matter?"

"Oh, I have a terrible feeling about this. I think it's best we leave right now. This place makes me nervous." Julia said, her voice pitched. "I've never been arrested before and I'd rather keep it that way."

"Come on, just a few more minutes, I promise, right after I have a look in the windows," I said, and Julia walked beside me sizing up the odd building teeming with possibilities as to what might be inside. At the window, we pressed our faces against the glass. Shadowy objects came into focus as our eyes adjusted to the darkened interior. I hadn't a clue what I was looking for since the contents seemed fairly typical, and what you would expect to see in any barn across rural America.

"See anything?" I asked Julia.

"Like what?"

"I dunno."

"Then why are we doing this?"

"I dunno."

"Here we go again. Honestly Molly Hanson, you drive me nuts."

"Wait, did you hear that?"

"No."

"The same sound I heard before." I put my ear to the sky, straining to understand the airy noise until it weakened and was gone for good.

"It could been a motor running or anything for that matter."

"It was there. I'm positive I heard it." I stood motionless, afraid I might miss the sound. "There it is again, listen," I whispered as steam rose from my breath. My ears snatched at the slight murmur splitting the cold air. It was faint but definite. "Can't you hear that?"

"No, Molly I can't. I'm leaving right now before someone calls the police on us." Julia proceeded to angrily trudge her way to the car. I wasn't far behind.

"What's the big hurry?"

"I'm taking you back to your crappy vehicle. You're on your own from there."

"Okay, okay, I get it. But let me ask you something first."

"No, I don't want you to ask me anything."

"Did you see anything interesting in the barn?"

"No, not really."

"Me either, just the usual stuff, a workbench, tools, gas cans, old bottles, mud bogging tires, and a rusty riding mower."

"Judging by the state of that yard, you have us exploring junk," complained Julia climbing into her car. Her tone made it clear her participation had come to halt. She was finished with me and my creepy house investigation. I dug around in my jacket for my pack of gum. There were now two pieces left in the pack. I deliberated again about giving up a stick, but figured our friendship was worth it.

"Want a piece of gum?" I asked, shoving a stick in my mouth, and chomped away like a cow chewing cud.

"Sure." Julia hesitated, and then accepted the piece of gum as a round-about apology, and just like that, peace was restored throughout the universe.

Friendships are weird. They come in multiple shapes and sizes, with some consisting of pure joy welded together by unbreakable bonds. And then there are other types of friendships, like the one I have with Julia, that are a colossal pain in the ass. Obviously, my role was playing the latter.

"Turn up here, Anderson Auto Body is on the left. Looks like they're not busy. Great, I won't be stuck reading greasy motorhead magazines for hours on end," I said, hinting for Julia to wait with me. But she said nothing and that made me very uncomfortable.

Julia rolled her car in front of the repair shop door, cut the engine, unbuckled her seat belt, then drew in a long breath preparing her lecture. "Molly, I have something important to say and it's imperative that you fully understand me for once. I know that you can't help it when you act the way you do, sometimes operating full tilt like a beagle pup needing a run, but you have to seriously think about your motive with this guy, and his house. You're pushing your luck too far and could wind up in jail, or with a criminal record. I'm saying this as your friend. Try to take into consideration how an arrest would reflect on your husband. You should think long and hard about my advice. What's the point of obsessing on this guy anyway?"

How was I supposed to answer when I knew the cold hard truth was that I might be the one who's responsible for the Gas & Go Mart girl's demise. I should have insisted on dropping her off someplace safe, but instead I took the easy way out. No doubt I'm guilty of being complacent and a selfish jerk. "It's just a hunch I have no choice but to follow through with," I mumbled, getting out of Julia's car.

"Molly, sometimes not getting what you want can be a form of good luck."

"Well, my luck's more like a bald guy who just won a comb."

"Just think about it, please Molly, it's for your own good."

"Alright, I'll try, but I'm not making any promises," I answered, and Julia released a sigh.

"I'll give you a call when I'm home, but not right away. I hope you don't take this personally, but I really need a break from all this chicanery. It's too much sometimes." Julia turned over the engine, then pulled away without a wave, or a honk goodbye, which lately seemed to be happening a lot.

As her new car ascended down the stone driveway, I reflected on my friend's words feeling like the buffoon that I truly am.

-twenty-two-

With my tail wedged firmly between my legs, I went inside Anderson's Auto Body repair shop. "How's it going, Al?" I shouted, letting the door slam behind me.

As usual, Al Anderson was sitting on his red vinyl covered stool, glued to a daytime television game show with the volume on high. Leftover coffee from the morning singed the burner, releasing a familiar acrid odor. The television audience applause, filled with cheers, brightened the dingy, grease-tinged waiting area. Al's moment for retirement came and went several years back. He'll never give up his shop to someone else. In all likelihood, Al will die under the belly of a car making a repair. Regrettably, the repairs on my van had provided a major contribution to his income.

Al looked up when I came through the door, "Where have you been, Molly? Your van's ready for you."

"I had to catch a lift."

"You weren't hitch-hiking, were you? It's a dangerous world we live in."

"No Al, nothing like that. How bad are the damages?"

"It's just a fuel pump, not too bad." He tore the bill from a grease-stained pad and slipped it to me across the counter. "The van shouldn't give you any more problems."

"Thanks Al," I sighed, taking in the grand total. I filled out the check for the repair, hoping there was enough money remaining in my bank account to cover the amount.

"You don't look so good," he asked. "Why the heavy face?"

"I'm starting to believe the biggest mistake I ever made was letting people stay in my life longer than they deserve to."

"Nonsense, it's rubbish to say such things. You're a good person. And I, for one, consider myself fortunate to know you."

"Al, if only you were ten years younger, and I was still single, you'd have some trouble on your hands my friend."

"Ah!" Al waved me off, slid the van keys my way. "Your van's parked on the side," he said, his attention back on his television program.

"Thanks again," I said, but he didn't notice. I walked around the side of the building to the van, wiping grease from the doorknob on my jeans. I climbed inside the van and inserted the key into the ignition giving it a hopeful turn. The engine started with a silky purr. It was good to be in control of my life once more. I phoned Hank, "I'm on the road again."

"I'll alert the media; they'll issue a public warning."

"You are so funny, and the bill Al just handed me was hilarious."

"How's the van running?" he asked.

"It's fine now. Al has that magic touch."

"You might consider upgrading to a newer vehicle."

"Julia says the same thing, but I'm fond of my van, and don't mind the smell." I've grown accustomed to my *Loser Cruiser* and its peculiar noises, offensive odors, and dried dog snot smeared

---

on the windows. Despite how everyone feels the need to express their derogatory opinions about my vehicle, I don't care. The van suits me. "I'm on the way home. Do you need anything?"

"No thanks, I'll see you tonight." Hank disconnected. I flung the phone on the passenger's seat and set my sights for home. Julia made sure to put an end to my adventures for at least one day. I turned off the highway, passing the sheriff's department and the creepy house and withheld my gaze from them both.

I am finished wasting time mulling over that girl, non-existent strange sounds, Camo Man and his stupid ugly house and his junk that multiplies daily. I bet he's a DC transplant. It's a common rumor that all Washington DC transplants are retired spies. Sure, its speculation, but it is a possibility. I have to admit it, I love riding the gossip train as much as everyone else.

I wonder how Camo Man had managed to snag a position at the county hospital? He would have to know someone higher in the hospital chain of command to land a respectable job like that. In Somerset County, the *good old boy system* has ruled since the beginning of time, maybe even longer. So, who gave Camo the leg up, and why? The bigger question is, do I have enough real estate left in my head to figure out the answer? You bet your life I do.

-twenty-three-

On Smithtown Island, the weather operates by its own rules at an unpredictable pace. I was reminded of that when crossing over the last bridge and took a direct hit from a hateful gust.

I veered onto our driveway and shut the van off realizing I didn't have a clue how I got here, being preoccupied to the point where I could have been ticketed for a driving-without-concentrating violation. Before going inside, I checked up and down the road. There was absolutely nothing happening. Compared to the busy metropolis of the outside world, Smithtown was several light years behind.

I hurried inside the house fighting against the wind to open the front door. "Anybody home?" I called, thinking the place was deserted until the dogs finally came. Rubbing my arms for warmth, I tapped the thermostat up a few degrees, then let the dogs outside for a pee, keeping an eye on them through the kitchen window. I searched the yard for any signs of life attempting to grow.

Surprisingly, my knockout roses are the only plant that can take a severe wind beating and thrive in post hurricane Sandy soil. For days on end the high tides saturated the ground and raised the salinity level that burned everything but my knockout roses. With their ability to tolerate the worst of soil conditions they would probably do quite well planted in topsoil from Chernobyl.

I was about to call the dogs back in when a tiny movement caught my eye. It was our neighbor crossing the road heading to her crab house with her orange striped cat following close behind. Born on the island, Alma Hicks had tended crab houses her entire life. Shortly after her husband had died from a heart attack, she began tending to her son's catch. Alma stands about four foot none, and wears an apron under her pale pink cardigan twelve months a year. Her hair, like everyone else's hair in Smithtown, was naturally highlighted by the sun except hers had a little gray mixed in. Like her ancestors, Alma is a hard worker, steadfast in her ways. During the summer crabbing season, her crab house lights stay lit late into the night as she cleans soft crabs. In the off season, she passes the winter months by assembling crab pots on her living room floor while watching her favorite television soaps.

Alma is as much part of the island as the air she breathes. She's friendly to an extent, sharing very few words and the occasional wave. After all, I am a come-here and it's best not to get too close to my kind.

At the back door shivering at the bitter cold, I was unable to wait any longer for the dogs and hollered for them to come inside. They quickly dog-obliged by trotting to the door, then suddenly stopped in their tracks distracted by a sound.

"Help, help me," a cry came from the direction of Alma's house. I looked over in time to see a windswept crab pot hurling end-over-end up the road. I went around the house towards the whimpering sound where Alma lay on the ground with her cardigan sweater and apron hoisted over her belly.

"Are you hurt?" I knelt down beside Alma, and so did Bam, kissing her on the mouth. "I'm sorry, he must have followed me," I said, pushing him away.

"My arm, I think it's broken. The wind knocked me down. It happened so fast."

"Let me get you upright," I said, slipping her sweater and apron back in place for modesty. "Your arm looks terrible. I better take you to the hospital."

"Just take me to the doc-in-the-box in town, the hospital is too far away," she said, writhing in pain.

"Where we live, everything's far away," I said, glancing at her swollen arm ballooning from her cardigan. "I think you should go to the hospital. Don't move, just stay put. I'll go fetch my van."

"Hurry," she grimaced, cradling her arm.

I ran across the yard, scurrying the dogs in the house and grabbed the keys to the van. Starting the engine, I punched the gas pedal careening the vehicle over the grass to the little body lying in a crumpled heap.

"There's a mattress pad you can lay on." I gently eased Alma into the van onto Sara Jane's arthritic pad.

"Oh, my arm really hurts," she groaned.

"You can use my coat for a pillow," I said, sliding the garment under her head.

"What stinks so bad in here?"

"It's my dogs," I explained, opening the window a crack. Alma's arm was the color of a fresh summer eggplant and yet still found it necessary to complain about the smell. There's no doubt that island women are grown from hearty stock.

Gently, I hustled Alma to the hospital, checking on her welfare after each pothole.

"Are you making out alright back there?"

"Yes, thank you. The pain seems a lot less now that my arm has gone numb." Alma shifted her body to a comfortable position on the dog bed.

I knew the numbness to be a bad sign and pushed the van harder. It retaliated with laborious moans as if it was giving birth to triplets.

"I'm sorry Alma, but my van just doesn't have any get up and go left. I'm going as fast as I can."

"It's alright dear just as long as we get there. I'm a little lightheaded that's all."

Great, that's all I need. If Alma dies on my watch, I'll be run out of Smithtown by torch fire and pitchfork.

"Hold tight, we're almost at the hospital," I said, flying up to the *Emergency Vehicle Only* sign. I knew Alma would receive attention by a professional much faster this way.

I pulled up to the emergency entrance and two physicians rushed through the automatic doors expecting an ambulance.

"Hurry, my neighbor fell and broke her arm. Can you help me get her inside?" I asked, then climbed in the van next to Alma. She was covered in dog hair.

"Did you say a sheep dog knocked her down?" asked the emergency worker, stretching blue latex gloves over his fingers.

"No, it was the wind." Embarrassment flushed my face red.

One of the men wheeled Alma through the emergency doors, as the other followed and pointed to a row of uncomfortable vinyl green chairs. "You can wait here. Someone will be out shortly to get her information."

"Where are you taking her?"

"X-ray. It's going to be a while. They're backed up from a five-car pile-up on the bypass," he said, rolling Alma through a second set of doors, and then they were gone.

"That's just great," I answered, looking around the room spotting two expired germ-ridden magazines, and a television tuned to the cooking channel missing its remote. I sat in one of the green chairs skimming the periodicals, *Popular Mechanics* and *Good Housekeeping*. I then turned my interest to the children's corner of toys and books to find that some kid already circled all of the hidden objects in a *Highlights* magazine. After five minutes of being subjected to the cooking channel, I thought I would die and dialed Hank, saying I was at the hospital with Alma.

"Is she alright?"

"I think she broke her arm. That woman is tough as nails."

"I'll call her son and let him know what happened. You should stay and wait there until he comes."

"But it's so boring."

"Watch some TV."

"It's stuck on the cooking channel. It hurts my brain."

"You can stick it out for a while."

This wouldn't be the first time Alma had to wait on her son to be rescued. Last Summer, she somehow got herself locked inside the walk-in crab cooler and had to wait five hours before being discovered. Alma turned almost the same color purple as her arm.

I took a deep breath, then let out a loud sigh. "I'm sure Alma has plenty of staff monitoring her every move. She'll be just fine by herself. I really don't need to be here."

"You'll be fine Molly. It was a good thing you did today, remember that." Hank disconnected. It's a rare moment when I agree with my husband, it was good of me to drive Alma to the hospital, but waiting in this dismal room was downright torture and not what I signed up for.

"Molly Hanson?" Towering in the doorway, a heavy-set woman dressed in navy blue scrubs recited my name from the clipboard she held in her plump fingers.

"Huh?" I replied.

"Are you Molly Hanson?"

I hesitated before saying, "Yes, I am."

"I have an update on Alma's condition. She broke her arm in two places, and we're keeping her overnight for observation. Nothing serious, a precautionary measure due to her blood pressure level being terribly high. We think the fall she experienced could be the culprit."

"Good news, I can go home now."

"She was asking for you."

"But you don't need me for anything else right?"

"She requested to see you." The woman raised a disapproving eyebrow.

"Alright already. I'll visit her, but only for a minute. What room is she in?"

"Room three-twenty-seven. The elevator down the hall on the left." She flashed a plump grin over her clipboard.

I took the elevator to the third floor and stepped out into the virus filled air. I walked down the hallway reading the list of room numbers, until reaching room three-twenty-seven and peeked inside. Alma lay in the bed watching daytime talk-show television with the blankets pulled tight to her chin and her new white cast resting gently across her chest.

"How did you manage to snag a private room?"

"It won't be for long. The hospital's overfilled with new patients. I heard there was an accident on the highway."

"Yes, a bad one. Good thing we didn't take that route."

"Molly, I want to thank you for taking me to the hospital. I know it wasn't easy for you."

"What do you mean it wasn't easy for me?" I asked, leery of where Alma might be heading.

"Acting kindly towards people."

"What are you talking about? I'm nice to people."

"Is that what you think? Besides today, can you name one selfless act, or when you've shown generosity towards another human being?"

"What makes you the big authority on my life?"

"I know everything dear. When you've been alive as long as I have, you come to understand the truth about people."

She had me on that one. I couldn't think of one example. Although, somewhere in my past life, there had to have been a kitten stuck in a tree I saved.

"Just because I can't think of any at the moment, I'm sure I have done something nice."

"Well, here's your chance for more. Go find a vending machine and bring me back a soda. There's money there in my purse," she motioned with her good arm at an end table next to a chair.

"Sure thing, but I'm buying. You can count that as two good deeds." I left her room searching for a vending machine, surprised I couldn't find one on the third floor, and took the elevator to the lobby where several vending machines lined an alcove. I fished through my pockets for exact change, then slid the coins in the slot and pushed the Coke button. Nothing happened.

"Shit," I groaned, shook the machine and gave it a whack and the Coke can fell from the machine with a thump to the bottom. I checked my coat pockets for additional coins, finding enough to buy a second Coke for myself. I pulled the tab open spraying sticky brown soda all over me and the floor. "Shit," I said again, wiping the soda off my coat, then checked to see if anyone was looking. I was all alone except for the sound of keys jingling.

I followed the sound to the other side of the lobby to where the hospital's janitor emptied waste receptacles humming along to a tune playing in his ear-buds.

Camo Man.

He methodically replaced the plastic liner inside a trash receptacle, then moved the cart on to the next. Recognizing who it was, my heartbeat raced, coursing blood through my veins. He wasn't the big hero Walt described. He wasn't mending the sick, or eradicating diseases. He was a mild-mannered janitor, the kind of janitor who spends his off hours involved in heinous unlawful activities. I'd bet my life on it.

My right eye began to twitch as strange feelings swiftly overcame my thought process. The Gas & Go Mart girl, trash truck, Camo Man and his creepy house sped in circles around my cranium, as the slightest cry played helplessly in my ears. I thought I was falling apart, possibly having a complete mental breakdown. I couldn't stop my eyes from fixating on the source of jingling. Camo Man had in his possession the keys to the kingdom. He had access to every room, office, prescription pad, and medicinal pantry. Invisible to hospital staff, he could effortlessly travel all around without being noticed. In essence, he owned the joint and everyone in it.

He looked up, narrowing his sight on target, which was me. My mouth flew open. Did he recognize me from the Gas & Go Mart? In a complete panic, I blazed a trail down the hall to the elevator, pressed buttons until the doors opened and I was safe inside, and called Walter.

"Don't hang up. I'm at the hospital. I ran into Camo Man."

"Hospital, what did you do now, Molly?"

"I'm fine. Listen Walt, it's important. Are you aware he has access to everyone and everything at the hospital?"

"Cut it out Molly, you're overreacting again."

"But Camo could be stealing narcotics in broad daylight and no one would be any the wiser."

"How do you know? Do you have any proof?"

"No, just a hunch."

"I can't do police work on a hunch." With a click, the line went dead, and not because the metal elevator interferes with cell phone reception, but because Walter's most favorite thing in the world is hanging up on me.

"You're such an asshole," I said. What was I thinking? No way would he listen to my theories. I need to hatch a better plan if I want to fry this embryo.

With soda in hand, I returned to room three-twenty-seven where Alma was now positioned upright in her adjustable hospital bed, lounging comfortably and watching a soap opera with her good hand clutching the remote.

"What took you so long?"

I opened the soda can and placed it on the bed tray, moving it within her reach, "You're welcome."

"My son is on his way. He'll be here soon so you can leave if you want too."

"No, it's alright. I don't mind waiting."

Did I say that out loud? I must be coming down with some sort of contaminant, a virus, courtesy of the hospital.

"Do as you wish," she said, returning her attention to the glitzy television actors.

I settled in the vinyl chair unconsciously mesmerized by the figures moving across the screen. I thought about Camo Man and the mysterious sound drifting from his creepy house, if I had heard anything at all. The house was old like mine. I could imagine it was just the wind whistling through the boards.

-twenty-four-

Forty-five mind-bending minutes later, Alma's son finally relieved me of duty. I couldn't drive fast enough away from the hospital, Gas & Go Mart girl, Amber Alerts, Camo-Man and his scary property. Breaking the speed-limit, and my all-time record for reaching home, I was able to enjoy the peace and quiet and a glass of wine, or two or three that would hopefully help me forget this day ever happened. If something else should land on my plate I might just dive into the deep end for good.

Soothed by a decent wine buzz, I listened to the wind while preparing another mediocre meal. Hank was seated at the table poring over the Somerville Times newspaper, occasionally glancing up as the gust raged on, ravishing the shorelines of the tiny island. It's expected that Smithtown winters will be dreadful, but why does it feel the need to test my worth? This is how I keep track of time now. Not by a watch or clock, or calendar, but by the earth's behavior within the seasons. With every peeler-crab run, rose bloom, and shifts in the sunlight hours I know what's coming for me.

The wind continued increasing in strength, blasting fearful blows against the house that rattled the structure with every hit. I knew the center of the storm was nearing and carrying a force behind it.

"It's a rough one out there. Going to get worse too. They say a Nor'easter will be here by early next week," Hank commented, totally unfazed by the elements hammering down on our house.

"Great, I can't wait," I answered. Hank grinned at my sardonic tone.

"Did you hear that, just now?"

"If you mean the wind, then yeah," I said, thinking it was a ridiculous question.

"No, not the wind," Hank remarked in a way that picked at my last nerve.

The wind paled under the noise of whooping helicopter blades piercing the night, whirling louder with each rotation. I shut the sink water off and looked out the kitchen window. It was just after sunset, when the sky bends into a deep Prussian blue in color, coating the last trickle of light. The machine's hum drew Hank to the front room where I quietly joined him.

"It's hovering over Prickly Point," Hank nodded toward the helicopter swaying against gusts. "I'll go find out what that's all about." He threw on the goose down filled hunting coat that hung by the door. Noticing the concern on my face he said, "It's probably nothing. I won't be long," then left the house venturing out into the blustery weather.

Filled by a familiar sense of hopelessness, I followed his silhouette move down the pier into the darkness. Tugging the wool blanket off the couch, I pulled it snug around my shoulders, then slipped on my white crab boots by the backdoor and went outside. The wind pushed at my back, knocking me off center, and I had to steady myself until reaching the end of the pier by Hank's side. The helicopter continued its vigil scanning the water, its beam skirting the edges of the land. Neighboring boats began to appear with spotlights also gleaning the Sound. The chopper suspended over the water, sending giant rings into the search field beam. Without faltering, the pursuit went on as the hours passed by. I knew their heroic efforts would soon be futile. No one could survive in this. The water temperature was dangerously cold and would cause hypothermia within minutes. This wasn't my first search rodeo, and sadly, it wouldn't be the last.

"It could've been you they're looking for." I held on tighter to my husband.

"But it's not." He squeezed my hand reassuringly, as if to convince us both that everything would be all right.

Hank wasn't the one who was lost out on the dark cold water. It was someone else's husband, and it was someone else's wife who waited for his return through silent, breathless prayers.

Life in general was challenging, with island life often excruciatingly demanding. It's not idyllic as portrayed in the theaters. It's a harsh and unforgiving treacherous land where one learns to exist within the environment, and develop an understanding of the destruction it randomly inflicts on the unsuspecting. And tonight, the elements had claimed the life of another waterman.

-twenty-five-

When I woke up, I heard nothing. No thrashing against the house, no creeks or moans. No noise of any kind. The air had stilled as if the wind gave up the fight. But I know better, it's resting now, back building for the next battle. The wind is relentless that way.

I sat up in bed and yawned. Bam was sound asleep next to me on Hank's pillow. I felt a twinge of jealousy at the dog's ability to fully enjoy a restful slumber. I slid my body upright and opened the blinds organizing the day's strategy.

I'll have to resort to plan B. Not having a plan-A in place is where I went wrong. Today I'm kicking ass and taking names.

Sara Jane, stretched out on the bedroom floor, tilted her head as if she understood my thoughts. I stretched and yawned again. I hate waking up tired. Hank tossed in the bed most of the night which meant neither of us slept much. It didn't help that the helicopter continued swiping the area until dawn, searching for a body with little hope of recovery. Having a waterman husband who faces dangerous conditions daily was something I've learned to accept. I find it best not to dwell on the negative or think about it at all.

Probing my closet for something to wear, I pulled out my old stand-by funeral pant-suit, the perfectly boring professional guise to steal my way into the Somerset County Hospital human resource department, for a non-existing job interview. Under the jacket, I wore a white V-neck sweater cut slightly too low, but not enough to be thought of as slutty, or distasteful. The last item I needed to pull-off this brilliant caper would be a touch of fire engine red lipstick.

Hopefully, nosing around the joint will unearth some dirt on Camo Man. Walter may think the guy is a harmless Girl Scout, but I suspect there's something rotten in his box of cookies, and I'm going to find out just what that is.

I brushed my hair into a tight ponytail, wetted down the flyaway stray strands, then applied the lipstick from a partially dried tube, a maneuver that I was obviously out of practice with, and had to rub the greasy red color off my teeth with my finger.

Before leaving the house, I let the dogs outside for their morning constitutional, then gave them both a pat on the head and a dog treat.

"Be good dogs, I'll be home soon," I said, then filled my crossbody bag with bare essentials for the day. I tossed in the one stick of gum left in the pack, my cell phone, two Twinkies, bottled water, and Hank's fishing magazine in case I might be required to wait an extended period. After my recent hospital periodical experience, I understood the importance of bringing my own reading material.

I checked my reflection in the hall mirror once more. I was pleased with my appearance even though my pant-suit favored Hilary Clinton on a Presidential run. At the front door, I stood a moment, questioning my motives. Okay, maybe I couldn't justify my next move, but I might find a way out of my quagmire of self-disappointment at my inability to act when I had the chance.

Wonder Woman wouldn't give up. I had to see this through and with any luck, I would discover the fate of the Gas & Go Mart girl, and possibly solve what happened to the other women who vanished into thin air. I turned the front doorknob.

While the van was idling in the driveway warming the engine, I sprayed Lysol over the interior to lessen the chance of foul odors latching onto my clothes. When the motor was ready, I pushed the transmission lever into drive, then rolled out onto the road leaving the island far behind with all the confidence I could muster. With any luck, this adventure could lead me closer to the truth. I hummed the Batman theme song blazing a trail along the highway leading towards Somerset Hospital.

These days, the only thing I'm able to accomplish is wasting fuel buzzing up and down this road. Today will be different after I destroy malevolent forces wreaking havoc on the world and prove once and for all that my instincts were spot on and that I'm not insane like Hank and Walter tend to think. I'll return from this mission triumphant and revered by them both and they will never disregard me again.

"I am Wonder Woman, hear me roar," I shouted, punching my fist into the air. Embarrassed, I put my hand down and headed back into reality, continuing quietly along the route to the hospital.

Cruising the multi-leveled parking lot, I nervously maneuvered the narrow turns until finding a space large enough to fit the van, then took the catwalk to the hospital elevator and pushed the call button. While waiting for its arrival several professionals, proficient in routine, had gathered alongside me. I straightened my back, hoping to pass as one of them. The elevator doors dinged open and we stampeded inside without acknowledging one another. I squeezed to the side, waiting until the elevator doors re-opened into the lobby, emptying its passengers who went off in separate directions without giving me a second thought. By all indications my plan seemed to be working smoothly and would be easy-peasy to pull off successfully.

Overhead, I found a sign specifying various hospital departments and floor locations, reading each name on the list, and spied *Billing Services*, room two-forty-two.

"Can I help you?" asked a woman's voice from behind a wooden kiosk.

I turned around, taken back by an overzealous makeup application, which judging by the thickness of her prescription eyeglass lenses, was due to her failing eyesight.

"Is there something in particular you're looking for?" she smiled, leaning over a laminate countertop. I noticed a name tag pinned to a flowered blouse that said *Alice*.

"I have a job interview with billing services."

"That office is on the second floor. You can take the stairs, or the elevator. You'll find it on the right-hand side. No one informed us that human resources were conducting interviews today. I thought the hospital had placed a freeze on hiring until the spring. Oh well, what do I know, I'm just a volunteer."

"And you're a fine one at that." I remembered Burton's advice when extracting information that a little honey goes a long way, and this small gem could be my honey hole.

"There's a new position in bookkeeping. I saw the position posted on the bulletin board when I was here last visiting a friend. How long have you been volunteering?"

"Over ten years now. I started soon after my husband died, he was ill for a long time. The hospital staff were wonderful. They took excellent care of him. I wanted to repay the hospital for all the kindness they had shown us," she explained, and I realized Alice was very much the chatty volunteer. I felt my hands sliding deeper inside that honey pot.

"That's commendable. Ten years is a good stretch of time. Then you must know everyone that works here," I said.

"Oh, yes, without a doubt. I know some better than others, certain types like to stick to themselves. You know how people are."

"Then you are the right person who can help me. You see, I had forgotten the person's name in billing I'm scheduled to see for the interview. I'm afraid it wouldn't make a positive first impression without it," I said, thinking I could do this all day. Off the cuff fibbing is high on my talent list.

"That would be Mr. Reid Roberts. He's in a meeting right now, but you can wait for him outside his office. He should be through shortly."

"Mr. Roberts, got it thanks. I remember the name now," I said. Liar, liar pants on fire.

I heard the jingling of keys and my head snapped around, following the tinkling echo slicing through the air like the sharpest of knives. Partially hidden by a potted Ficus tree, stood Camo Man on the other side of the lobby, and he wasn't alone. In what looked to be a stolen moment, he held the hand of a nurse in her mid-twenties. She nervously glanced around, then hastily kissed him. And just as quickly, they parted and Camo Man carried on with his janitorial duties.

"How about him, do you know that guy?" I asked Alice.

"I know all the hospital employees, and that will include you as well if you are hired for the bookkeeping job. What's your name dear?"

"Molly. What about that guy, what's his name? I think I might know him." Careful not to cause suspicion, I treaded lightly, keeping her chatty. "He wears a camouflage coat just about every day of the year."

"That's Gordon Myers. Nice young man despite the coat."

"I'm sure he is," I said agreeably, but wanted to say, *Yeah, right. He's a real prize idiot.*

"He starts his morning shift with a polite smile."

"What about that nurse, do you know her?"

"I already told you I know everyone here. You sure ask a lot of questions."

"I just want to be prepared if I land this job. I'll be required to keep track of all department employees."

"Yes, I see your point. It's Dorothy Wills. She's fairly new, started about three months ago in general nursing. She used to work swing-shifts. Recently, they moved her to the pharmacy where she has a nine-to-five position. She's not as social as he is, and acts a little uppity if you ask me."

This was adding up fast, but to what, I wasn't sure of yet. The Camo Man had a pharmacy nurse as his girlfriend, who had access to the pharmaceuticals, and he had the keys to everything else.

My initial investigation has ended successfully for now. I still need to find out more.

"Good luck with your interview."

"Huh, oh, thanks Alice. I better go now. It was nice to meet you."

"You as well. Remember, second floor and stay to the right."

"Yep, thanks again." I didn't fancy the idea of getting sweaty climbing steps and opted for the elevator instead, taking it to the second floor. *Muzak* edged through the speakers playing soft rock tunes. Yikes, not my favorite genre. In less than a minute the doors dinged open. I stepped out checking the hallway, then strolled down the corridor past two guys in uniforms who were busy fixing the water fountain. I hurried by tilting my face, obscuring any identifiable features, a technique I retained from watching television detective shows. I followed Alice's directions and found the door marked *Billing Services* in gold lettering, then plopped down in one of the three available chairs in the hall. Although I knew better, I began perusing through the hospital magazines sitting in a woven basket to discover they were all of the boring medical variety. Why personnel would think that the non-medical population would find that sort of reading appealing was beyond me. Good thing I came prepared. I fetched the Rod and Reel magazine from my handy bag of tricks and started skimming the articles until hearing footsteps trodding down the hall.

I glanced upward to see a man in a pale lemon yellow short-sleeve shirt, brown tie, pants, and shoes, unlock the door and enter the office. By the looks of this guy, the door sign should have read *Loser Nerd*, instead.

I tucked my fishing magazine away, brushed dog hair from my suit, then gave a confident knuckle wrap on Reid Robert's door.

"Come in."

"Hello, I'm Molly Hanson. I'm applying for the bookkeeping position. I hope it's still available." Without invitation, I made myself comfy in a faux suede chair, then batted my eyelashes while flashing a come-hither smile.

"Bookkeeping no, simple filing yes, but I'm afraid it's only part-time. I've had trouble filling the position, the pay is minimal, and there aren't any benefits to speak of, except for the accidental death policy which doesn't cover papercuts. I wasn't aware human resources had posted the position."

"The job sounds perfect and just what I was looking for," I said, then leaned forward hanging on every word and exposing a little cleavage to boot.

"Do you have experience? I know it's totally unnecessary to ask that question. Formality habits die hard, I suppose. Putting records away isn't complicated, you don't need any experience. When can you start? Are you married?"

His face glazed over and I knew he was mine. As he rambled on about the filing system, I nodded periodically, feigning interest and let my eyes roam past a stack of business manuals lining the shelf behind Reid Roberts head, and down to a tall mahogany file cabinet containing personal information on all hospital employees right down to their shoe size. I needed to get my hands on it, but how I would gain access had turned into a stumbling block. Suddenly, an idea came to mind and I started to cough, and then choke.

"Oh, my goodness, are you alright? Can I get you a drink of water? There's a fountain just down the hall. How about I bring you some water?"

"Yes, please," I coughed again, knowing perfectly well the fountain down the hall was out-of-order, and that Mr. Reid Roberts would have to go to another floor to fetch the water. I wouldn't wash my hands in that bacteria infested, hog trough of a fountain, leave alone drink from it.

"I'll be right back, don't go anywhere." Roberts grabbed the stained coffee mug sitting on the corner of the desk, blew dust from the inside, then rushed from the room.

Even though Roberts looked a bit out of shape and would need the extra time to complete his task fetching water from another floor, I knew my file cabinet pilfering opportunity would be short lived and hurried, thumbing through the human resource employee files, desperately searching for the name Gordon Myers. The musty files reeked from the overstuffed antique wooden cabinet. Halfway through the letter *M* section, I found what I was looking for and began to speed-read through the list of Myers' previous addresses. His last location was listed in DC. I knew he had to be a transplant. Under his work experience, Gordon Myers named several menial jobs, nothing alarming jumped out at me. His background check was marked *Cleared* in red ink. That's impossible. Someone must have fudged his files. It's the only way he could procure employment at the hospital with a prior criminal history.

I jammed the file back inside the mahogany drawer, slammed it shut, and gathered up my belongings. I needed to go before Roberts conjured up the wrong idea about me. I left the office, moving at a fast pace down the hall passing by a confused Mr. Reid Roberts.

"Later man, got to run," I said in flight.

"Wait, what about your water? I still need additional information. Are you single? What's your number? Tell me your phone number so I can call you sometime," he cried out, slowing his pace.

I thought it possible that Sad-Sack Roberts might call security and took the stairs to the lobby, which made slipping undetected by Alice manning the kiosk a piece of cake. Luckily, Camo Man was nowhere on site.

I would say the mission couldn't be more successful than it was, and that I'm fairly skilled at undercover work. The next time there's a job opening at the sheriff's office I think I might give it a shot. Who am I kidding? I wouldn't last three minutes on the job with Walter as my supervisor without killing him first.

-twenty-six-

I set off, cruising down the highway, destination home and a big, fat glass of wine. I realize that some people might consider the late afternoon as an unacceptable hour for consuming alcohol, but I never gave a rat's ass what other people think.

Besides I deserve a drink. After all, I am one puzzle piece closer in solving the riddle. Too bad I won't be able to share my enthusiasm with Hank, or impress him with my ingenious investigational skills. I would make an awesome detective, or a Walmart security guard using my powers to bounce people out of the twenty-items-or-less line for carrying twenty-one items. Someday, when I have all of my life's ducks in a row, I'm filling out an application for a law enforcement position somewhere.

One-hundred yards past the *All-Points* sign, I veered off, taking the shortcut connector road where I spotted the trash truck parked outside of Camo Man's house. If I had any sense I'd pay no mind to the situation, but considering I'm not one for choosing the right path, I slowed the van into the sheriff's department parking lot and shut the engine off. With an unobstructed view, I scanned the area, checking on the chicanery brewing directly across the street.

Right on cue, the driver lifted a large plastic bin from the passenger's side of the truck, then carried it around to the other side of the house out of sight. I closed my eyes desperately trying to connect the dots until they blew apart, fracturing into a million tiny bits of nothing. I heard the man return to the truck and rev up his diesel engine. I shot up in the seat wondering if I missed the big moment I came for.

As I heard the story later, inside the sheriff's building, a large woman became annoyed when eyeballing the rusty white van parked in the lot. "Better come out here and have a look at this, Walt," she casually shouted at the rear part of the office. Rita had been the sheriff's department dispatcher for longer than she cared to admit. In her many years as a department employee, she has seen and heard it all, and had more than her fill. When it comes to the ins-and-outs of her office duties, Rita's abilities were beyond proficient, and just like Walter, she wasn't fond of me either. Rita was a barrel-chested woman who towers over most humans on the planet, and on more than one occasion had boobie-bumped me out the office door.

Walter meandered over to the office front window, peered between the gold window lettering at the department lot and sighed. "Oh, for cripes sake Molly, what mischief have you gotten yourself into now?" He rubbed his face contemplating if he really wanted to know the answer.

"I'll be right back Rita, this won't take me long," he sighed again.

"I doubt it," she snickered.

Walter stepped back inside his office to shut down his favorite video game on the department's computer, then pushed his comfortable ergo dynamic office chair under the desk, the one he specially ordered on the Amazon website. He inhaled a deep breath, then crossed the parking lot and tapped on my van window.

My heart turned over in my chest.

"What do you think you're doing? You scared me half to death."

"The question here being, what are you doing, nothing above suspicion, I bet."

"Please Walt, listen to me for once. Take a look at that guy driving the trash truck. I just saw him carry a big plastic tote around to the rear of the house a few minutes ago. I'm telling you that some sort of depravity is running rampant inside that house. I'm right about this, I'm certain of it. Why can't you see it all happening right under your nose?"

Walter looked over at the house but by then the trash truck had driven away. "I don't have a clue what you're talking about. I think you better come inside the office for a minute. I have something you should see. You're making yourself upset over nothing," Walter pleaded. "I'm asking you to come inside and hopefully put a stop to this madness once and for all." He turned around heading to his office, hollering out, "You coming or what?"

"I suppose so," I answered, exiting the van, then shuffled behind Walter through the sheriff department's front doors where the office pit-bull was waiting with arms crossed.

"Rita," I nodded to her.

"Molly," she smirked.

Walter ambled down the hall to the rear office, "Sit here next to me."

THE ISLAND STOOD STILL

I slid a metal folding chair squealing across the linoleum floor and sat down, "What's this about?"

"Hold on a minute, I'm pulling it up now" he said, leaning over his computer typing a few phrases on the keyboard.

"This better be good."

"Have a look at this." On the state's criminal background website, Walter opened a file on Gordon Myers, certain the information would convince me to give up the ghost. "You can see with your own eyes, no major criminal offenses listed, just a couple of misdemeanors and a home foreclosure procedure notice issued six months ago. He's drowning in a load of debt, but that's it. Myers moved to Somerset County for the same reason as everyone else, because it's an affordable way of living."

I re-read the file's information twice over until my eyes began to dry up. There was a ton of information listed on Myers, none of which would help my case. I was so off base I might slip into another world dimension.

"This should satisfy your curiosity," Walter noted, pleased with himself.

"Wait, this can't be all there is," I said, and just like that, I was plucked back into earth's gravitational force. "Do you know why Myers is working at the hospital, besides the great pay, health benefits, and the matching retirement plan?"

"Where's this going Molly? Never mind, I really don't want to know." Walter rolled his chair facing me.

"I bet you didn't know Myers has a girlfriend that also works at the hospital."

"That means diddly squat. Most couples meet through the workplace."

"What if that girlfriend happens to work in the hospital pharmacy? Wouldn't that make it simple as pie to pilfer pharmaceuticals by intentionally making a mistake here and there in the orders? With a hospital position like that nobody would suspect drug theft. Think about how the illegal drug sales would bring in a tidy sum and pay off Myer's mounting debt. What do you think about that, Walt?"

"Oh, give it a rest Molly. Get in your van and take that rusty eyesore out of here. Go on home to your husband and leave this alone. We're done with the insanity portion of the show." Walter shook his head, raised himself from his desk, and showed me the door.

"Nice seeing you Molly," Rita smirked again.

"It's been a real pleasure, Rita," I sneered at the two of them. Walter's futile attempt to steer me off the course of my mission was useless. My fixation was unshakable.

I moved the van from his department office lot, just as Sheriff Fat-man requested, and parked in front of the creepy junk-ridden home where I sat stewing in my own juices. The gray weather had cast a veil over the premises in what felt like something eerie looming. Whatever it was, I could sense it in my bones. I got out of the van and quietly closed the door. I stood firmly on the roadside, confronting the ugliness in the air and, for a brief moment, I could swear I heard a faint cry riding on the wind.

Through the department's office window, Walter pinned a watchful eye on my movements as I climbed back into the van and flipped him the bird, then headed for home on my own terms.

-twenty-seven-

Vehicles zoomed in the north and south bound lanes completely clueless about malicious events running in full operation as oblivious as Walter seemed to be. Then again, there are some advantages to living with your head buried up your bum. I'm jealous of those who can.

Stopped at the highway entrance, I took a guess which direction the trash truck chose to travel, picking the northbound side of the road. I pushed the rusty gas pedal to the floor and hauled the van in hot pursuit of the smelly vehicle. Heeling the white whale of a van into the fast lane, I paid no mind to the blast of car horns, and kept my eyes peeled, scanning the asphalt lanes up ahead for the trash truck.

Sunlight flickered through a thicket of pine trees separating the four lanes as a safety barrier. I sped past, avoiding a strobe effect headache.

Because of its weighted load, the trash truck moved at a slower pace making it easy to spot. I caught up in less than a minute. The truck turned off the main road and so did I, staying far enough out of sight. The truck slowed, and then stopped at a rundown farmhouse belonging to the Sun Solar Savvy Company. Before the property was covered in solar panels, it was once used as farmland for many generations and had acres of beautiful green fields, rotating crops seasonally. There was a time when golden sunflowers grew along the edges swaying against the breeze. Now, the farm's crop yield consists of chunky metal and plates of blue glass. I understand the importance of advancing technology, and the use of alternative energy sources for the sake of the earth's health. But I don't understand why the solar companies never considered grazing cows under the solar panels, perpetuating the charm and integrity of farming life.

I pulled over to wait for the trash truck by the small water treatment block building where the van would be invisible. It wasn't long before I saw black smoke puff from its underbelly as the truck returned up the lane. The driver finessed the lumbering vehicle back into traffic, coaxing the struggling motor. As planned, the driver didn't notice my van hidden by the building, or when I slid in tight behind his truck. Following a vehicle this closely is dangerous, and certainly illegal, but in this position, I was able to hide the van in the truck's blind spot. The truck resumed his route and I kept glued to the vehicle's rear-end. I didn't have a clue why I was following this truck. I also didn't know what I would do when it stopped.

This might be the stupidest thing I have ever done in my life, or at least it ranked high on the list.

At the Somerville intersection, the traffic light signaled a change from a yellow warning to red. The driver manhandled the truck, Jake-braking the cumbersome beast to a halt. I slammed on the van's brakes; it squealed in retaliation, almost plowing into the rear of the hydraulic trash compactor door. At the risk of asphyxiating because of the idling diesel engine fumes, I opened the window gasping for a breath. Ten seconds later, the light turned to green and the driver accelerated the truck, packing the van with a full blast of toxic engine fumes. This was ridiculous. I veered off, taking the Main Street business route through the town of Somerville, thinking that someday I may have to get a real job and give up my monkeyshines altogether, but not just yet.

I cycled through my mental list of suspicions, sectioning hard evidence from circumstantial. In conclusion, it was my sanity that was seriously in question. I had zero solid evidence to go on. The house was creepy, big deal. So, what if Camo Man dated a nurse. It's not a big deal being friendly with someone who drives a garbage truck. The only real facts I had was that it was me who was breaking the law, not Camo Man. Breaking and entering and trespassing on private property is illegal. I could very well be arrested and end up upsetting my husband forever, and that was the most unfortunate factoid of the day. My plans had turned into a total bust. My head felt the same way. The only remedy for achieving mental redemption was perusing the local wine collection, refurbishing my stock.

I parked curbside, adjacent to the Somerville State Liquors. Approaching the store front, I felt my mouth salivate imagining popping the bottle cork. I opened the door to the boozer and a small cowbell rang, announcing a customer.

"Hi Molly," hailed a thirty something woman behind the counter. I was thankful to see buck-tooth Bonnie and not the owner of the liquor store who is meaner than a paper bag full of snakes. On the other hand, Buck-tooth Bonnie was as sweet as homemade ice cream on a summer afternoon, and completely comfortable with her facial malformation. The same goes for her husband, who seemed totally oblivious to Bonnie's excessive tooth deformity, and also of their six buck-toothed children's inherited affliction.

"What's shakin, Bonnie?" I asked.

"Nothing new ever goes on around these parts, just the same old grind, dull as dishwater. You want the usual?" she asked through a toothy grin, reaching for a bottle of white wine.

"Yep, same thing, chardonnay please." I replied, thinking why did my life always play out like a cartoon strip?

"Here you go." Bonnie placed three bottles of wine, separated by cardboard partitions in a plastic bag, then rang up the tally on the vintage register. "Anything else I can get you?" she asked, handing over the receipt.

"Nope, thanks. That will do it for now." I paid my bill, then gathered the wine, bottles clinking inside the bag despite the cardboard. "Nice to see you again Bonnie," I said as I turned towards the door. Out on the street, the trash truck driver emptied the trash receptacle, then setting it to the curb with a bang, moved on to the next overflowing trash can. The noise cornered my attention.

"Nice to see you too, Molly."

"Actually Bonnie, there is something else I need. Would you happen to know anything about the driver of that truck?" I asked. The one thing I have learned throughout my years was that the local boozer was a sure-fire wealth of information.

"Oh, I know him, not personally I mean. He comes in here frequently."

"What juicy bits did you notice about him?"

"I've mostly seen him at the Relax Inn Motel."

"No kidding? What do you think he's doing there?" I asked knowing it sounded like a dumb question.

"Nothing good from what I hear. I would know. I can see everything that goes on there from my house."

"I see what you mean." I wondered if Bonnie could hear the loud ticking inside my head. The driver was definitely involved in something, most likely illegal.

Bonnie leaned over the counter and whispered, "And get this, each time he's with a different girl, blonde, redhead or a brunette. Every time he's with a different woman, but they all have one thing in common."

"Oh, what's that?" I whispered as well, though I wasn't sure why Bonnie thought it necessary since I was her only customer.

"They're drunk off their asses and can barely walk from the truck to the motel room."

"Drunks of a feather drink together," I said, aware that I didn't have room to comment on someone else's drinking habits. Apparently, I visit the liquor store often enough that Bonnie knew me by my first name.

"With as much alcohol as that man buys, it's good for business."

"Thanks Bonnie, I better be getting home."

"Sure thing, Molly."

After loading the wine goodies safely in the van, I turned the key then continued home, examining the conversation with Bonnie. Her observation about those women struck me as odd that she automatically assumed they were intoxicated. But then again, if the trash truck driver was trolling for women in a bar, then yes, the likelihood they might be high or smashed would

213

make total sense since Ranks Bar was only two short blocks walking distance from the no-tell-motel. The bar had a reputation for catering to a fairly dicey clientele since the first day of operation and continues receiving various fines for serving alcohol to minors. Ranks is also known as a popular place for drug arrests by the Somerville police.

I ran up on the trash truck again as it waited at the traffic light to change color. Go figure. That's how my luck rolls. The decision to continue tagging behind the truck would be ludicrous at this point, but I never have listened to my better judgment before, so why start now? For miles I stayed hidden, lagging several car lengths behind the truck, until the driver angled the rig into the guest parking lot belonging to the Relax Inn Motel and stationed the big diesel truck by a guest room door.

There he goes, just the way Bonnie told me.

I parked the van under cover by the dumpster where I could smell the rot even with the windows closed. Yes, it was another dumb move on my part, but the Relax Inn Motel was best known for its hourly room rate and I couldn't risk being spotted by the driver, or by any other Somerset County resident for that matter. Explaining to Hank as to why my van was parked at Somerville's infamous love huts would be a tough one for him to swallow.

Keeping a bead on the driver, I was able to fully evaluate his features. He was tall with a large frame, and he had a sway in his gate that favored his right side. As he meandered towards the row of motel room doors, he paused at a door with peeling paint, then fiddled with a large key ring fastened to his belt. Finding the desired key, he unlocked the door and stepped inside the room.

I don't think I'll ever understand the fascination men hold for their overloaded key rings. I'll have to ponder that another day, right now, I have a million questions hurling against my forehead.

It's pretty obvious why the driver was at that motel room in the middle of the workday. He wouldn't be the first to enjoy a little afternoon delight. From what I could tell about the driver's appearance, he'd have to pay a professional for that sort of service. Prostitution would be a better answer, and the Relax Inn would fit the bill perfectly. It was the type of motel where you wipe your feet on your way out.

As much as I didn't want to, I knew there was only one solution that would reveal the exact criminal enterprise the driver was tangled in. I closed the van door quietly then inched across the lot to the motel room window and pressed an ear against the glass. Though unclear, I heard voices behind the dingy curtain. Ironically, I didn't have a problem deciphering the angry shouts rising in volume behind me.

"Hey you, get away from there. I called the police." The motel office door flung wide open and a man came out waving his arms in the air. He ran down the walkway and I turned tail to my van, started the engine, and flew from the parking lot before I was arrested on several counts of voyeurism.

"You pervert!" the agitated man shouted after me.

The motel owner's assessment of my behavior would be considered accurate by most people. I felt a little ashamed. Without a doubt, the incident wasn't a high-point in my life, although it did make the low-point list with honors.

-twenty-eight-

I checked the clock. It was quarter to nine. Hank had turned in for the evening an hour ago. He didn't say much over dinner. He was too tired to learn about my day, and I was grateful for not having to fabricate one.

The last thing my husband needs in this world is hearing about what I've been up to.

I thought it was best to end on a high note and joined Hank upstairs. Bam jumped in the bed between us and took to snoring as fast as Hank did. I lay there listening to their esophageal chorus, waiting for sleep that refused to come. For me, restful nights are extremely hard to come by, particularly with a fretful festering mind. I was in for another exasperated night counting the vintage bedroom asbestos ceiling tiles watching animal forms appear in the textured design. Lying wide awake night after night is agonizing. Sometimes I believe my insomnia is punishment for something I did in my past life.

The wind was gaining in power, stressing the clapboard. I tossed on the bed for another hour listening to the wind hurl sticks and pine cones at the house before giving up on sleep altogether. I went downstairs and flicked on the main light, illuminating my neglect in every room, the whole place was in serious need of tidying. I bet Wonder Woman never concerned herself with such idiotic chores.

Being the size of a shoebox, the house didn't take much effort or time to clean. As a reward, I poured myself a glass of wine and began tooling around on the internet which killed an additional half-hour. I pressed the television remote on and channel surfed for ten-minutes, nothing caught my interest. I did find plenty of infomercials and shut down the television before I bought something ridiculously overpriced again. Mixing wine with impulse purchasing proved to be extremely dangerous to my wallet.

The wine did little in coaxing the rest I yearned for. I climbed back into bed and closed my eyes, completely powerless in putting a halt to the parade of Gas & Go Mart girl images marching behind my eyelids. She's somewhere out there now, cold, hungry and frightened, then again, she could also be someplace with her feet propped up and watching television. I squeezed my eyes tighter until the little girl with the red ribbon withered into nothingness.

I should have done more, I thought, sitting up and moved to the edge of the bed. Beads of sweat formed over my forehead, and my chest felt like it was pinned under a pile of bricks. Maybe this was how a panic attack feels.

I lay back down on the mattress, bringing my breathing under control. There was no need in waking Hank because I was in the throes of a meltdown. If I could just forget about the girl, then all would be right as rain again. She was never my responsibility to begin with. It's the authorities' problem, not mine. Horrible things happen everywhere, every day, every minute, and every bit of it was beyond my control. But people don't just disappear without a trace, not without leaving some indication. There had to be a sign.

I sprang straight from the bed, landing on my feet like an Olympic gymnast. The motion stirred Hank and he rolled over falling deeper into a slumbering state of contentment.

Tip-toeing around the room, I dressed in the clothes I had tossed earlier on the floor, then threw on a black hoodie and zipped it closed. Hank snored, practically comatose. Bam, on the other hand, was alert, keeping a steady eye on me. I went downstairs to the front door and grabbed my winter coat from the hook and then stepped out into the cold dark night. The air stung my face and lungs. The wind blew with an intensity sent straight from the north pole. I slipped inside the van and held my breath, slowly closing the car door. Shifting the gears into neutral, I let the rusted white whale roll backwards down the driveway before kicking the engine over, sneaking away from the house as if I'd practiced the maneuver a thousand times.

I stayed put in the road, calculating my next move. The temperature was bitter cold, enough to see my rapid breath. My hands were shaking on the wheel from the icy conditions and nerves.

This would have to be the craziest idea I ever concocted yet. Hank would kill me if he knew what I was about to do. I don't care. There was a sign, plain and simple and obvious as a sledgehammer to the forehead. I'm positive beyond all doubt that I had heard a strange noise come from inside that house. Even though Walter, Julia and Hank may think I'm crazy, I know what I heard. I'm certain of it.

I knew my chances of this harebrained scheme ending successfully were slim-to-none, but it was the only option. I put the van in gear and drove down Smithtown Road, watching the house porch light dim then fade in the rearview mirror the same way the Gas & Go Mart girl dwindled into the night. The van sped around the marsh, further away from the safety of the island with each winding turn.

On the mainland, riding along on the dark stretch of road under a vast and starless sky, my tension mounted. Coming up on the open twenty-four-seven Gas & Go Mart neon sign, I was guided by the light shining brighter than all the casinos in Las Vegas stacked together.

I slowed, passing the store, there wasn't a car in the lot. Inside, the building showed empty, except for the night clerk engrossed on his phone. I rolled around the corner onto the connecting road, then cut the lights and parked the van. My cell rang and I almost threw it out the window. The caller ID said it was Megan and I let it go to voicemail and turned the ringer off like I should have done before I left.

Whatever my sister wants will have to wait. I'm on a mission.

On the left side of the road, the Sheriff's Department sat cloaked in darkness, indifferent to what transpired across the street. I glanced up at the creepy house. There was something different about it, sinister in appearance and completely unnerving. Trees surrounding the dwelling swayed in the advancing wind, its waving branches beckoned for me. Apprehension gurgled in my abdomen and I thought a piece of gum would placate the sudden gastrointestinal needs. Slipping my hand in my pocket, I plucked out the packet of Juicy Fruit gum. *Damn,* it was empty.

Scoping out the property, I noticed Myers vehicle wasn't in the driveway. His absence would work perfectly in my favor. Exiting the van, I waited a few minutes until my eyes adjusted and the random forms assembled into sensible objects in the shadowy atmosphere. Further up in the yard, I saw a sliver of light streaming across the tall dead grass and felt compelled to go towards the barn where the light had originated. My instinct indicated it was all right to investigate. No one would be able to spot me trespassing around the property under the invisibility of the night. I moved in the direction of the barn with mindful steps crunching over the frozen ground. As I walked, I suddenly became overwhelmed by an unfamiliar sensation, and then realized that I was scared. Blood whooshed, pulsating a steady rhythm behind my ears. Hyperventilated breaths wheezed through my opened mouth. *You can do this* I thought, and continued stealth-like through the area, careful to avoid bruising my shins on various ominous metal objects.

Passing the house, I saw a soft light emanating from the kitchen and thought it must be a night light. Strange, I didn't peg Myers as one who cared about ambient lighting. I decided to have a quick look and stooped low until reaching a window and stood to have a peek. Instantly, my eyes cut to a pile of keys on the kitchen table, the very same keys I heard jingling at the hospital. Growing footfalls resonated inside the house and my heart felt it would explode. Camo-Man, Gordon Myers, flicked on the kitchen light and fished out a smaller set of keys from the pocket of a coat draping a kitchen chair. After selecting a single key, he turned towards the back door and I hit the dirt face first. Myers wasn't supposed to be home.

I must be blind as a fruit bat to miss his coat hanging on the chair. Myers turned the knob, and I knew I would be as good as dead if he saw me. I had to act fast and ran through the yard, falling down behind a small bulky wooden structure. Judging by the stench it was the dog coop belonging to his nasty mongrel.

I heard Meyers' boots pounding the ground, gaining in volume as he stomped on by. All my survival instincts screamed to high-tail-it home to Smithtown, but Wonder Woman would be so disappointed if I bailed now. I had no choice but to see this through, and let my common sense fly out the window at warp speed.

I followed Myers from the house to the barn where he used the smaller set of keys to open the door. I waited until he was inside before making my move. Whatever that would be, I didn't know yet. Hiding in the shadows, I now understood why Myer's car was missing from the driveway, as I watched him unload several boxes from his vehicle and then carry them inside. Trying to decipher the writing on the boxes, I remembered that optometrist appointment scheduled over a month ago I didn't keep.

Myers returned to the car once more, grabbed the last box and closed the hatch. This was my chance. Slouching, I scooted across the grounds to the barn, then peered in the window. On the rear wall, a collection of chemical weed killer containers lined the shelves, which judging by the overgrown property, had never been utilized. Below the shelving, Myers was busy washing multiple items in a laundry basin. He repeated the process, then neatly placed the cleaned objects on a metal tray lying on a wooden workbench. Next to the tray sat three medicinal dispensing vials, identical to those I've seen in hospital television shows. That rat-bastard. I knew Myers was ripping off the hospital. Straining my eyes, I focused on the contents of the tray. Hypodermic needles were placed in a neat row like tin soldiers poised and ready for action. Myers was engaged in something dreadful. I was certain of it now.

Piercing the stillness of night, a cell phone rang and I almost fell over from fright. Myers answered on the second ring. Cradling the phone steady in the crook of his neck, he spoke while methodically filling the hypodermic needles with the contents of the glass bottles.

"Uh huh, they're starting to wake up. I'm preparing another dose, should be last of the evening. They'll be ready for you in the morning. Yep, same time, see you then," Myers confirmed, and then disconnected.

My mind felt heavy knowing whatever smarmy activity Myers was stirring needed to be put to an end. It was up to me to stop that man. Freeing my cell phone from my pocket, I sent Walter a text.

I need help.

In seconds I received a reply. *No.*

I sent another text message. *I need back up. Call the police.*

He responded with. *Leave me alone.*

I typed in all caps. *HELP ME NOW.*

New message, *No way Molly.*

Michele M. Green

I gave it one last shot typing - *BIG FAT JERK FACE,* and in return I received a silent response. I was on my own. Tears of frustration began to swell and I wiped them away. This was not the time for sentiment. I ran to the house, reached the back door and turned the knob. I couldn't believe Myers had left it unlocked. I stepped over the threshold, illegally entering the home and became acutely aware with heightened senses. I felt the structure creaking underfoot as I moved through the main room and down the hall. This time around I was seeing the house through a keener eyesight and noticed Myers maintained his home meticulously neat. How did I miss that factoid when snooping around the premises before? But then again, I was more preoccupied with fear of having my face ripped off by that ugly dog, than grading Myers' housekeeping skills. It was then I remembered his disgusting varmint was in the house somewhere. My vision darted around the immediate area, and then down the hall. The coast was clear, no indication of the ugly dog anywhere. I needed to hurry. Myers could come back inside any minute.

I proceeded to go deeper into the depths of the house. I saw flickering green hues along the hallway wall, then remembered the bare lightbulb in the pool room and went inside where I heard a faint, but distinct desperate moan. Snatching the syllables from the air, I moved to the far end of the room and placed my fingertips on the rough surface of the false wooden door. Cautiously, I asked, "Hello, is anyone there?"

-twenty-nine-

"Help me," came a slight breathy voice filtering through the door.

Startled, I fell backward.

"Please, help me," the voice said again.

Scrambling for a knob, I ran my hand over the door, "I'm going to get you out of there," I responded, and the voice from the door began pleading.

"Please, you have to help us."

"Hang on, I'm trying to open the door." I pulled on the door, but it was dead-bolted shut, just as before. I started to panic. What was I thinking? I can't do this alone. Then it hit me. Myers' big key ring was lying on the kitchen table. I ran back to the kitchen, snatching the keys off the table, and then ran down the hall to the poolroom's locked door. With shaky hands I rooted through the ring, desperately searching for the correct key that would release the dead-bolt.

"Please," the voice cried out again. "Please help us."

"I'm trying," I said, in a strained voice because I had stopped breathing several minutes ago.

"Get me out of here. I want to go home."

"Stand back from the door," My hands trembled, jingling the keys.

"Please," the voice cried in jagged sobs.

"Come on, come on," I repeated, inserting each key until finally the lock fell away. With all my strength, I pulled open the painted wooden door, and then my reality switched into slow motion, my reasoning slurred. The acrid stench of body odor exploding at my face kicked in my gag reflexes. I turned my head trying to understand what was happening. I thought maybe my eyes were playing tricks, because this couldn't be real. I must be dreaming.

"Will you help us?" asked a young woman, her body quivering from head to toe.

I was stricken by an atrocious smell emanating from the darkened room, and froze in place as my mind began to comprehend this secret chamber. Windows were boarded over with rough-cut planks to block the daylight from entering. The single source of light came from a fluorescent bulb that highlighted the horror in grotesque contrasting forms. Mounted near the corner, a small greasy sink and a toilet set on a damp cement floor where murky water puddled towards the center. In the middle of the nightmare, four more young women lay on soiled canvas cots, completely unaware of their surroundings, almost as if they were sedated. Their odor was nauseating. *Oh Myers, you monster, what have you done?* I brought my hand to my forehead. This was all so insane. The only explanation that would make any sense is that I'm in another dimension spinning through a black hole vortex.

"Try and remain calm, everything's going to be alright." I spoke in a soothing tone of authority to alleviate panic, but I could smell their terror in the air, and on me.

If Myers comes back, we're all dead. My attention snapped towards a high school aged girl, who had bruising on her left cheek, sitting immobilized on a stained mattress. She looked up and I thought she had a strong resemblance to the Widow Stone's granddaughter. Then I said her name.

"Rebecca, Becky Stone?"

"Yes, it's me. I want to go home. Will you take me there, please?" Dried tears stained her dirty face.

I moved towards the girl and gently touched her shoulder. "Everyone is going home, but we have to leave right now."

A third girl, not much older than Becky, drew herself upright, then sobbed into her hands.

"Get up. Myers went to the barn. We don't have much time before he returns. Go wake the others, we have to move, hurry," I said, hoisting the girl up on her feet.

Fear filled her eyes "No I can't, you don't know what he'll do to us if we misbehave," she cried.

I put the girl's hand in mine, "Tell me your name?"

"Natalie."

"We have to leave right this minute. Do you understand me? You can do this," I said, seeing her not as a woman, but a little helpless girl. Somewhere out there, people were worried to death over this girl. A sudden burning fury transformed my thoughts into angry bitter sharpness and I never felt more alive or sure of anything in my life. I knew what had to be done. With unwavering determination, I placed my hands gently on her cheeks and looked directly into her eyes. "Listen to me Natalie, you are the bravest person I've known. You're going to be fine, and so are the other girls, I'll make sure of it. But I can't do that without your help. Are you ready?"

The girl sniveled, "I think so."

"Then come on, let's get the rest moving." Commanding the situation, I began shaking the other girls, arousing them from their drowsy cots. With the women now mobile, I coaxed their weakened bodies down the hall towards the kitchen exit, with Becky heading the line.

"Thank you," she whimpered with a petrified expression.

"It's going to be alright, just keep moving," I said knowing Myers was only a few steps away. "Almost there," I motioned in the direction of the kitchen when that tangled haired dog materialized in the hall blocking our way. He bent his lips revealing his teeth, as a guttural noise escape his gooey mouth.

"Shut your face or I will kick your teeth in," I snarled, and the mutt scampered to the room from where he came.

"Keep moving, but be as quiet as you can. Stay close behind me." I whispered, leading the girls through the kitchen and then the back door. It was much colder. I knew the women's clothing would be insufficient in this weather. "This way," I pointed across the field at the patch of woods to where a beacon of neon light shone through the treetop branches.

In open fields the wind was unfettered by objects and grew in force. I was taken back by how roughly it tore across the field, the same way as it does on open water.

"I'm freezing," spoke one of the girls, hugging herself to keep warm. This worried me. They might panic and shut down completely.

"We'll make a run over the field to the woods. The Gas & Go Mart's on the other side. You'll be safe there. But you have to run as fast as you can and don't stop until you reach the store." I knew the field's furrows and frozen weed spikes would prove treacherous, maybe impossible to traverse for these frail women without twisting an ankle, but we had no choice.

"I can't make it," wept the smallest woman.

"You have to. Hold onto each other's hand, follow me, and don't fall behind." I took off for the field, running towards the woods with the girls scrambling after. Terrified and cold, they ran.

"Keep going, we're almost there."

The women began to scream in unison as horrifying shouts echoed across the field. Myers was on the hunt. His mounting rage wove between their frantic cries and the smashing of frozen ground.

"He's coming," someone shrieked.

"Don't look back," I yelled over my shoulder, relieved all five were still there. "Hurry, run to the light."

I ran faster than I ever have in my life. It felt as if my feet were flying until suddenly, I was stricken by a painful shock that punched all the air from my lungs. In the darkness, I hadn't seen that the field was separated by a tidal ditch. Icy water stung my head, as if bitten by a thousand wasps. Brutal daggers of pain seared my bones.

"Wait, stop. Don't come any further," I breathed sharply, struggling to gain a foothold on the slick crick bottom. I was swiftly sinking into the mud and buried my hand into the side of the embankment, steadying my stance. I reached out as far as I could. "Give me your hand and I'll help you across." The burning water temperature was spreading rapidly to my hips, jerking my body in shuddering waves.

"No, I can't, it's too cold," feared the first woman.

"Yes, you can. Take my hand, hurry," I demanded, my words slurring and I wondered why I sounded intoxicated. Stretching my deadened fingers, I grabbed her hand, dragging her and three more girls across the water, then one by one, heaved their wet bodies slipping up the embankment.

"Go now, run and don't look back no matter what you hear." They ran together, their silhouettes fleeing towards the safety of the convenience store, all except for one who wouldn't budge. "Come on, give me your hand."

"Promise you won't let go," she whimpered, latching her fingers into my hand but I didn't feel her touch. Numb to the core, my body was shutting down.

"Reach for the side, you'll have to pull yourself up," I gave one last push and the girl clawed her way over the freezing, muddy edge. "Go on now. Follow the others until you get to the store. Don't stop for anything," I whispered, slipping further into the water, sinking into the frozen blackness.

***

"You need to get up now, Molly. Wake up or you'll be late for school again," stated my mother, as she moved around my bedroom picking up dirty laundry from the floor.

"Mom?"

"Come on, sleepy head." She kissed my forehead with an easing warmth.

"I don't want to go to school. Why do I have to leave?"

"Everything will be alright sweetheart, you'll see. I'll be right here waiting for you," My mother offered her warm hand, and I reached out, joining her hand with mine.

***

The words *You need to get up now* pooled in my consciousness. My rising body swirled in a rush, breaking the water surface, drawing oxygen into my lungs. My hand stretched into the air, searching for something to hold onto, grasping for a root jetting into the embankment. With my last bit of strength, I kicked and pulled myself over the side, rolling onto the ground where I lay in the cold in a semi-conscious state. Relentless pain singed my nerve endings. I opened my eyes, Myers was nowhere in sight, and neither were the women. I prayed the empty field meant they had made it through the woods and safely to the store. I closed my eyes listening to my breathing slow in rhythm, slower still, until all light faded away.

-thirty-

As I gradually regained consciousness, I began to recognize the low muffled sounds as voices chirping through police radios. My body ached more than the worst hangover I ever experienced. Blue and red lights spun behind my eyelids. I was afraid to open them until I heard Hank say my name.

"Molly? Molly, are you alright?" his warm hands grasped my shoulders.

I sat upward, resting on elbows and opened my eyes. I was a little dizzy. "Hank, what are you doing here?" I was on the ground lying on an itchy gray survival blanket with a second one over me for warmth.

"Walt called me, right after you sent him an SOS text."

"Why?" I asked, confused about everything. "Where is he?"

"Over there," Hank gestured behind me. "He's with the officers interviewing some guy. Oh Molly, thank God you are alive." Hank tightened the blanket around my shivering body.

I heard the police talking and leaned my head sideways looking past Hank to where Walter and several of Somerville's finest hovered over a man also wrapped in a blanket.

Gently breaking from Hank's embrace, I whispered, "I'll be right back."

"What do you mean? Where are you going?"

"It will just take a minute."

Hank refused to let go of my hand, "Aw you know not, Molly, no, please don't."

"I need to know what happened to the women. Where are they?"

"They're at the hospital being treated, just like you should be," Hank remarked, completely undone. I tried standing and he swiftly responded with a firm tug on my arm, "No, Molly."

"Let me go, I have to go talk to him."

"Not until we check you out, miss," insisted a male paramedic who then proceeded to prod my body and wrap a blood pressure cuff around my upper arm. I heard whooshing as he rapidly pumped the ball.

"Stop that nonsense. I'm fine," I interjected, and pushed his hands away.

"Molly, let the man do his job." Hank, completely exasperated, stood with his hands on his hips. "Why do you always insist on acting so stubborn?"

"I'm telling you I'm fine," I said, wrapping the blanket around my shoulders. I'll be right back," I faked a pathetic smile assuring my bewildered husband as I walked away. I felt Walter's disapproval burn a hole in my back as I limped over to my hitchhiking Santa, who sat on the ambulance tailgate under the watchful eye of several police officers.

"Good thing that guy came along when he did. He can't be all that bad," an officer commented. "Hypothermia can come on real fast, and you could be deader than a nit in minutes."

Walter shot him a look.

"Ain't that something, he's just another homeless person. I've seen him around town a couple of times," remarked another policeman.

"Me too," added a third policeman. "The guy checks out, has a clean record."

"Would you mind if I spoke to him alone?" I asked one of the officers.

"We're done here, take all the time you need," he replied, then flipped his pad closed. He was old-school like Walt, I thought.

"Molly," said Walt, "I think it's best to stay at your husband's side. Look at him. Don't you see that you put him through enough already?" Walter nodded discreetly at Hank, whose anxious face now had contorted into deep wrinkles.

"I just need a minute Walt, that's all," I pleaded.

"There's no point in arguing with you." Walter threw his palms up. He went by Hank's side watching my movements like a hawk.

I lowered my body down on the ambulance bumper, next to my hitchhiking Santa whose eyes no longer twinkled.

"The girls, are they alright?" My ears were still ringing from the cold water, and a migraine headache was beginning to settle in, but the girl's welfare was my first concern. "Did they make it to the Gas & Go Mart?" I asked, still disorientated about the events.

I must be in shock.

"Yes, they made it, thanks to you. You're lucky you didn't die saving them," he noted, then shuddered under the blanket. So, did I.

"I don't understand. It's like you appeared out of thin air. The last time I saw you was at the bus terminal. I thought you said you had to go north for work." I didn't mean to badger the man, but I needed answers, and I needed them now.

"Yes, I did say that. I also told you I come from a place far north of here."

"That doesn't matter. What were you doing at the creepy house?"

"Watching out for you."

"But why?"

"I wish I knew the answer," he shrugged. "It's like something was guiding my way to you." He gave me a smile, one that felt warm and familiar, the very same smile I remembered as a child sitting on Santa's lap at the department store downtown.

This can't be happening.

I glanced at Hank who seemed comforted by Walter, doing the job of his best friend. I suppose in the big scheme of things; their friendship wasn't so bad after all.

"Looks like my work is done here." The hitchhiker said, snapping his body upward, letting the blanket fall to the ground. With a nod and a wink, he slipped from sight into the bleakness of the cold night, and for the first time in my life I had nothing to say.

"Can we go home now?" Hank's voice cracked. He was exhausted, and it was all my fault. What have I done to this man, the man I would marry a thousand times over, the man I love so deeply that sometimes it hurts? You would think by now I'd recognize how much I have to be thankful for in my life.

Suddenly several news vans rolled in with reporters exiting the vehicles before coming to a full stop, like lemmings abandoning a ship. This was the last thing in the world I wanted, or needed to deal with.

"Yes, please, I want to go home more than anything," I answered, really meaning it this time. At this point, a little island isolation with a side of boredom may not be such a bad thing.

-thirty-one-

White noise thundered throughout the house. Hank had set the television volume high enough to kill off several basilicas in both of my ears. Minimizing permanent damage, I turned the level down to an acceptable limit. I should have stayed in bed with my head under the pillow deep in denial, but avoiding the truth was virtually impossible, not with the local gossip seekers wanting to know about the sordid details.

I don't wish to be the central player in a local drama. I just want to forget about everything that happened and move on, but now, I get to relive the horrific event reported live on the six o'clock news.

Standing in front of the creepy house, the woman reporter listed the sordid details. I hung on her words like my last breath depended on it, and in some ways it just might.

Three people were charged on several counts of human trafficking, kidnapping, unlawful imprisonment, and illegal possession of large amounts of Dexmedetomidine. The Somerville Police were led to the suspects' home where five of their victims had escaped capture before they were transported and forced into domestic servitude. The female victims were rescued after being located inside a hidden structure at the suspects' home, where they were sedated and threatened physically if they tried to escape.

Hank came into the room, turned the television off, and then slid his arm around my shoulders. "Walt mentioned the hospital will provide the girls with all the necessary services for a complete physical and psychological recovery."

"Uh-huh," I answered, immediately remembering the repugnant stench after opening the painted door. Strange how quickly the body will turn on itself.

The camera cut to photos of the three suspects, Myers, the girlfriend, and the trash truck driver. I turned the volume higher.

Two of the suspects were employed at the Somerset County Hospital and have now been terminated. They were arrested after attempts to flee the area had failed. Authorities believed sedation pharmaceuticals used on the victims were illegally obtained through the hospital pharmacy.

The third man arrested orchestrated the kidnapping by luring young women into his Sanitation Department vehicle, then delivering his victims to their captive destination. Authorities say the investigation revealed the extent of the operation to be greater than originally suspected involving several states, and will be conducting additional arrests.

"You're nothing but a giant bag of anal leakage, Myers" I hissed at his photo, my cheeks flushed in anger. The sight of Myer's face summoned that same deep rage inside of me. Hank held on tighter to my twitching body.

The camera panned over the mounting crowd. The woman reporter shoved her handheld microphone into a man's face. He was taller than most, and wore a deep-blue suit and a red tie. I assumed he was politically affiliated, some town official. He stepped up to the podium, tapped the microphone, then cleared his throat before speaking.

"The Somerset County District Attorney's Office has been informed of the situation, and will offer full support throughout the investigation. The disturbing events occurring at the Relax Inn were highly suspicious, and should have been evident to the proprietors of the motel, yet little effort was made to stop the events from taking place. Owners of the motel are now facing charges for their involvement as accessories in drug and human trafficking operations. Somerville will never tolerate crime of any kind in our community. Authorities will continue doing their best in keeping our residents safe."

Reporters hurled questions simultaneously at the befuddled man. An officer intervened by stepping closer to the microphone. He began to read from a sheet of paper clutched in his hand, and a hush fell over the crowd.

"The Somerville Police have released the names of the five victims." Those words silenced each tongue. As he read the survivor's names aloud, photographs simultaneously splashed across the television screen, photos taken before the kidnappings, before their lives were torn apart from what they understood to be true in the world. I thought of the Gas & Go Mart girl and felt heartsick that none of the names on the list belonged to her.

"I can't believe this happened in plain sight, right across from the Sheriff's Department. There must be a whole slew of people involved in this," Hank said. "Oh, and just wait until I talk to Walt, I'm going to give him an ear full of crap. Who knows where those women would end up if it weren't for you, Molly."

"I wouldn't be so hard on Walt. He was working on the case, and knew more than he was willing to admit. The difference is, he has to work within the confines of the law, and I don't. His hands are legally tied."

"You're right, I won't mention it to him then. But still, it was right there across the street. Wait a minute, did I just hear you stick up for Walt?"

"I knew they were up to no-good. All three of them, Myers, the trash truck driver, and that nurse."

"Ain't that something? Nobody suspected a thing."

"What do you mean nobody?" I shot a wounded look at Hank.

"Sorry about that. I meant other than you." Hank went to the counter and poured out two glasses of wine, then set one down on the table for me. He turned to leave the room, stopping to say, "Come on hon, shut that noise off. It's Christmas Eve. Those girls are out of harm's way now, you need to leave that all behind and come have a cocktail with us." Megan was in the living room. He ran a reassuring hand over my shoulder.

"Sure, I will in a sec, after I catch the news," I replied, returning to the broadcast. I wished for a miracle that her name would be spoken in connection to the case. It was Christmas after all. Desperately, I waited for her picture to pop up on the screen, but there was no mention of Gas & Go Mart to satisfy my conscience. In all likelihood the girl was probably fine, and perhaps lucky not to be counted in the group of victims held against their will. I can tell myself these things until I'm blue in the face, but in reality, I knew the chances of her being in a non-threatening situation at the moment was fairly nonexistent. I took a deep breath to ward off the despair creeping in like a dense fog, then shut the television's power off. "I'm so sorry," I said to the blank screen. I had to let her go.

I can't live like this anymore. It's over, no more doom and gloom, and definitely no more grieving.

I left the kitchen and went up to the bedroom. Inside the third dresser drawer, buried under a stack of wrinkled T-shirts, was a photo of my parents that had the ability to cause a painful emotional rollercoaster ride with any glance at it. I took the photo out and brought it to the front room placing the picture on the end table. I let my fingers graze over their figures.

"Nice photo," said Hank looking over my shoulder. "I don't remember seeing that one before." Hank handled the photo, scrutinizing the black and white image. "They look so young, don't they?"

"Yes, they do. It's my favorite. It used to hang in my parent's bedroom where you wouldn't have seen it. I nabbed the picture from the house before it was sold."

"Does your sister know you have it?"

"It's not like I stole the picture. Besides, I don't care if she does know. Megan claimed everything at my parents' house."

"Didn't your sister peel back the wallpaper searching for hidden money?" Hank chuckled, at least he could laugh at it. Soon after my mother's passing, Megan removed all of the house items, furniture, heirlooms, and keepsakes that weren't nailed or permanently fastened, keeping it all to herself. It was as though the stuff held our parent's spirit, their essence. Ironically, hoarding their belongings did little in consoling Megan's grief.

"Shush now, she might hear you," I whispered, nodding towards Megan who was totally absorbed in hanging rescued Christmas ornaments from our parent's attic on tree branches.

"Don't tell me you're okay with what she did?"

"It's not even worth the trouble thinking about it," I answered, referring to my sister's difficult behavior that I've pretty much had to tolerate my whole life. Megan was a rebellious hippie chick, a product of her environment, like others in that age bracket, determined to rile against the establishment. Unfortunately, the majority of her grievances were directed at me. We fought constantly and drove our parents' nuts to the point they pretended we didn't exist at times. Sometimes. I used selective amnesia to survive and hid those useless emotions far enough inside me that you'd have to take my shoes off to find them. I find it's the best coping mechanism when dealing with the past, that and of course, alcohol. White wine is particularly effective for any ailment, except for the occasional suppressed memory stored in areas of my brain I can't control which seeps to the forefront when I least expect. I suppose that is where The Gas & Go girl will reside for the rest of my life, torturing me at random.

"I apologize if my inviting Megan to spend Christmas with us will cause more problems between you two," Hank said. Under different circumstances, I would have been furious at my husband for not consulting with me first. But after what I just went through almost freezing to death, I could care less. I am so over it. It doesn't bother me a bit that Megan made off entirely with everything my parents owned in this world. To me it was just stuff. Besides, my parents had already taught me what really mattered in life long ago. And most importantly, they showed me forgiveness more often than I deserved.

"No, it's alright, Hank. I honestly believe Megan's attempt at mending our relationship is genuine. The only way to freedom is to forgive. Many years have passed since my sister held a pillow over my face. I know it might be hard for you to understand, but I think I'm finally ready to let all that residual resentment go." I glanced over at Megan and the tree's transformation, shining in all its splendor in white twinkling lights through long aqua-green pine shads.

Hank had cut down the Leland Cypress in the woods where he hunts deer. The sappy turpentine filled the whole house with a scent that could turn even the Grinch into a sappier, holiday spirited version of himself. I was not in the proper mood for celebrations, or decorating, and was grateful that Megan took over. How could I celebrate when the Gas & Go Mart girl was out there somewhere? I would be more than okay with forgetting Christmas altogether this year.

"This looks just like the tree we had when we were kids," Megan expressed her excitement in an ear grating squeal. She smiled; her face reflected in bright tree lights.

As Hank handed Megan the extra glass of wine, I headed for the kitchen to make sure that wasn't the last bottle. In a small house such as ours, I couldn't help but overhear Hank saying, "I appreciate that you could join us for the holiday. I'm worried about your sister. Molly has wrestled with more than her fair share of close calls, and made it through without a scratch, but it's different this time. I think she's having a lot of trouble getting past this ordeal. I don't know how she's managing to keep it together the way she has."

"Molly always was the strong one. Gravity never could hold her down. She'll be alright soon enough, you'll see," Megan said, offering assurance placing a soft hand on Hank's arm.

I was surprised by Megan's uncharacteristic description of me, which I found it strangely comforting. For a long period of my life, we lived estranged from each other, and yet now it seems as if we never parted ways.

"I need her just as much. There isn't anything in this life more important than family," Megan asserted.

"That's true, although one should never overlook the importance of wine," I added, interrupting their discussion. The tree cast kaleidoscopic shades over the room. I lifted my glass toasting the two of them, and let the Christmas magic work its wonders. There was an air of easiness surrounding us, as Hank and Megan slowly sipped their cocktails. I chugged mine.

"Do you remember dad and that hulking thirty-five-millimeter movie camera he used to film us opening Christmas presents?" Megan quizzed.

"How could I forget those blinding floodlights?" I squinted at the memory.

Megan meticulously placed the last ornament on the tree, stood back and asked, "Do you think it's too much?"

"No, it's perfect," I commented, reaching under the tree for a small wrapped box and placing the present in her hand.

"What is this?"

"Before you open it, I need to tell you something, something I think is important. I want you to remember mom and dad as the kind and loving people they were, and that they're with you always, right there in your heart," I spoke the words that all grieving people want to hear, hoping it was true.

"Thanks Molly, that helps more than you can imagine."

In her excitement, Megan tore the Christmas wrapping off the gift in seconds. "You're kidding me. Where on earth did you find this?"

"Online of course, where else? I found the vintage Fuzzy Wuzzy Bear soap in mint condition while surfing the net." How strange the moment, being without hesitation or regret, I willfully hugged my sister.

I must be coming down with an illness.

"I love you too," she smiled.

I think memories are subjective interpretations riddled with holes that become increasingly inconsistent over time. I realize my sister and I experienced completely different childhoods, and each was extraordinary in their own way. The one absolute truth I hold near is the fact that we were both loved dearly by our parents.

Hank returned to the kitchen, refilling his bourbon on the rocks, and came back with the wine bottle that I'd dug out for him to find, rectifying my empty wine glass situation.

The doorbell buzzed. I went and opened the door to see my husband's best friend still in his uniform duds, and hid my disappointment

"Walt," I nodded.

"Merry Christmas, Molly."

"Merry Christmas to you too, I suppose. You're not thinking about hugging me now, are you?" I asked with uncertainty after my recent display of emotion with my sister.

"Not a chance."

"Good, for a moment there I was afraid you might," I closed the door behind him, grateful that some things never change.

The doorbell rang again, setting the dogs into a full-blown fit. I opened the door again and several of Hank's watermen friends filed into the front room in an abundance of boisterous chatter. Hank offered a round of beer to all, then immediately began to enthrall us with the latest hunting adventure. I retreated to the kitchen where the sound faded to a din. I wasn't up for a big crowd of people and preferred to observe the merriment from afar. It was odd to me that not one person seemed to have a care in the world, and I wondered if it was remotely possible for me to ever feel like that again. I doubted it.

I was filling my arms with various brands of beer when the doorbell rang for the third time. The dogs barked wildly. Hank, busy entertaining the masses, looked to have the situation under control, so I answered the door once again.

"Get back," I told the dogs, then turn the doorknob and was caught off guard at seeing Alma standing on the porch with her white plaster cast suspended in an orthopedic sling, and a young woman at her side.

"I'm surprised to see you, Alma, come in." Not only did I think her visit was weird, I was certain that nothing good would come from it.

"I will, but only for a minute. I need to have a word with you. This here's my niece, Lena. She'll be looking after me for a until my arm heals."

"Hello," I responded, blankly.

"This won't take long." Alma fiddled with her hand straightening her cardigan, a sure sign that an extremely uncomfortable situation was about to commence.

"What is it?" I asked, bracing myself for the worst.

"I've been thinking about what you did for those girls, I mean the way you helped them. You saved their lives. What I'm trying to say is, you're not as bad as I thought."

"Gee, thanks, I guess."

"I spoke my mind and said all I came here to say. I'll be going now."

"Wait, won't you stay and have a glass of wine, or a cocktail? We're celebrating with an impromptu Christmas party."

"Need a hand, Molly?" Wearing a goofy look on his face, Walter abruptly pushed me to the side and made a bee-line for Lena. "Hello there, I don't believe we've been introduced. I'm Walter, won't you come in? Can I get you a drink?" he asked, practically falling on top of the woman.

"Oh, I couldn't," Lena answered.

I almost broke out laughing at the smitten fat-man. Resurrected from the dead by an infestation of the love-bug. I held back the urge to tease Walter about guffawing over Lena. Afterall, this might develop into a serious relationship and I would gain my husband back.

"Why don't you stay, have a little fun," Alma winked at her niece, and then turned to me. "Thank you for your kind offer, maybe another day, dear," and with that, Alma was gone.

I gave a sideways glance at Hank, who looked about as shocked as I was at Alma popping up on our doorstep.

"I don't think I'll ever understand the Smithtown natives," I shrugged with palms up.

"You may be wrong about that. Alma appears to be coming around. I think she likes you. Big-doings for Alma to actually step inside our house. Who knows, she might even become your new best friend."

"Lord, help me," I muttered in defense.

"Here, I forgot to give this to you. It came in the mail today." Hank handed me an envelope postmarked from Florida. Curious, I pried at the edge, tearing an opening, plunged my hand inside and pulled a postcard. I read the handwritten message, *Merry Christmas*, then turned the card over, completely taken back by the photo. I felt a strong sensation of warmth melt over me and thought I might be glowing brighter than the Christmas tree.

"Can I see it?" Hank questioned. "I'd like to know what could make you this happy."

I handed Hank the postcard. After analyzing the photograph, he turned the card over and read the message.

"Who are those people?" he asked, puzzled by a photo that planted a joyful, beaming grin across my face.

"It doesn't matter, you wouldn't know who they are."

"Alright, if you say so, then I guess it doesn't matter. Whoever they are, I'd like to thank them."

"I hope that one day you'll have the opportunity. Stranger things have happened." Studying the photograph, I released a large breath and all my anxiety with it, and all it took was a picture of my hitchhiking Santa sitting in a beach chair with his toes in the sand drinking margaritas with the girl from the Gas & Go Mart. I fought back a tear that managed to escape my eye and let it roll freely down my face.

"This was by far the best present I ever received in my entire life. All the girls are safe. I know that now," I said, slipping the picture back inside its envelope.

"What are you talking about Molly? There's nothing for you to worry about."

"I know," I said, squeezing Hank's hand.

With the second round of cocktails consumed, the party hummed higher. I reached for my handsome husband, pulling him close.

"Are you alright Molly?"

"Yes, I am now, perfect in fact. I finally figured out that all you need to get by in this life is to have a little faith that everything will turn out fine, in this world and in the next."

"What did you say honey? It's too loud, I can't hear you."

"Oh, nothing," I smiled and kissed my husband as if it was our first kiss. Hank slid his hand under the backside of my shirt, then planted his lips hard against mine, sending a heatwave all the way south of my border to Hoo-ha-ville.

Michele M. Green is a professional artist, musician, and author, whose work is inspired by foot, boat or kayak, and as a result has an intimate and personal relationship with her surrounding landscape.

She had been a frequent contributor to *Outdoor Delaware Magazine* and her work is popular in many prominent collections, including the collection of President Joe Biden. Michele is also a member of the Eastern Shore Writers Association, and a committee member for the Maryland Humanities *One Maryland One* books.

Michele resides on an island with her husband, and her two dogs, one cat, and a parrot that curses like a long-shoreman on weekend leave, in the lower eastern shores of Maryland, where she writes her Molly Hanson mystery novels.

You may contact Michele at greenbanjo@hotmail.com

Acknowledgments

I am forever grateful for my parents, Nancy and Richard Green, who showered me in praise and encouragement by treating every little piece of junk I created since birth as masterful works of art. I hope I still make you proud, wherever you are.

To everyone at Blueberry Lane Book Publishing, you rock! Thank you for all that you do in bringing the Molly Hanson Mystery series to life.

I'm so thankful for such organizations as the Eastern Shore Writers Association. It's comforting to know that there are other like-minded lifeforms out there wandering around the universe.

The Island Stood Still was originally written on an old crappy laptop with the letter Q cap missing from the keyboard.

If you enjoyed reading The Island Stood Still,
please consider leaving a book review on Amazon.com
Thank you for supporting the arts.